"What's the matter? Have I got my hair mussed?"

"No, I shouldn't think you ever go into public without a careful perusal of your toilette from all angles," she retorted, piqued to have been caught out in her examination.

"Very true. I have been pirouetting in front of my mirror this past half hour, and can't think what detail escaped me."

"No detail. I have been admiring your barbering."

"May I return the compliment and say I admire your coiffure? *La Greque* suits you very well." Monstuart took care that no hint of admiration lit his eyes, or lightened his bored tone. "You are wise to continue wearing it, even though it is no longer considered the highest kick in fashion in London," he added.

Miss Hermitage was not deceived into taking this for a compliment. Like any provincial lady, she was sensitive to the charge of being behind the style. His sly setdown was as good as an invitation to battle.

Also by Joan Smith
Published by Fawcett Crest Books

BABE
IMPRUDENT LADY
AURORA
LACE FOR MILADY
VALERIE
THE BLUE DIAMOND
REPRISE
WILES OF A STRANGER
LOVER'S VOWS
RELUCTANT BRIDE
LADY MADELINE'S FOLLY
LOVE BADE ME WELCOME
MIDNIGHT MASQUERADE
ROYAL REVELS
THE DEVIOUS DUCHESS
TRUE LADY
BATH BELLES
STRANGE CAPERS
A COUNTRY WOOING
LOVE'S HARBINGER
LETTERS TO A LADY
COUNTRY FLIRT
LARCENOUS LADY
MEMOIRS OF A HOYDEN
SILKEN SECRETS
DRURY LANE DARLING

THE HERMIT'S DAUGHTER

Joan Smith

FAWCETT CREST • NEW YORK

A Fawcett Crest Book
Published by Ballantine Books
Copyright © 1988 by Joan Smith

All rights reserved under International and Pan-American Copyright
Conventions. Published in the United States by Ballantine Books, a
division of Random House, Inc., New York, and simultaneously in Canada by Random House of Canada Limited, Toronto.

Library of Congress Catalog Card Number: 88-91301

ISBN 0-449-21588-1

Printed in Canada

First Edition: January 1989

Chapter One

Mrs. Hermitage raised her elbow and gave her elder daughter a surreptitious poke in the ribs. A toss of the mother's head and the language of the eye told Sally the lovers by the grate were to be left alone. Not loath to abandon such dull company, Sally picked up a magazine as an excuse to move far across the saloon to a reading lamp. Within seconds Mrs. Hermitage took her netting box and joined her. A certain smiling unsteadiness around the elder lady's lips gave rise to wild hopes.

"Has Derwent come up to scratch, Mama?" Sally asked eagerly.

"The thing is as well as done." Mrs. Hermitage breathed a sigh of exquisite relief. She stole a glance to the grate and a tear misted her eye. Melanie, her favorite though it would never do to say so, looked like a princess from a fairytale. Firelight shimmered on her blond curls and caressed the perfection of her profile as she gazed steadily into the eyes of her Prince Charming, Lord Derwent.

"It will be the salvation of us, Sal. Such shallow

waters as we have been swimming in since your papa went and died on me."

Dying prematurely was the meanest trick ever played by Mr. Hermitage, a man who was infamous for his tricks. Sally had been just on the verge of coming out four years ago when her father had played off his last stunt. She certainly would have nabbed a parti. The family lived in high style in a fine rented mansion on St. Charles Street and knew everyone. No thought of future penury ever bothered the Hermitages. Papa was the outstanding solicitor in the city. Members of Parliament and peers consulted him on their more arcane problems. Drawing up a will or a marriage settlement was nothing to him. He handed it over to one of his many minions and busied himself with weightier stuff.

A noble estate whose ownership was in question, or some complicated government matter, was what he considered worth his time, both financially and mentally. The Hermit, as he was called by the legal world, had been that rara avis, a legend in his own lifetime. It was said he had the keenest legal mind in England and could charge what he wished for his services. He charged plenty, but still the spending of his wife and his two daughters had managed to put a hole in his earnings.

"Did Derwent speak to you? Did he make a formal offer?" Sally asked her mother.

"No, *in*formal. He must speak to his uncle first."

"Lord Monstuart," Sally said. Her pretty face hardened at the name.

Looking at her, Mrs. Hermitage was extremely grateful that her younger daughter had brought a

2

gentleman up to scratch, for it was far from certain her elder would ever accomplish such a feat in the provinces, despite her looks. Her jet-black hair, her green eyes and trim figure hadn't won her a single offer. There was just a certain something in Sal that put the local men off. Her brasher style would have taken in London, but it had not taken in Brighton or Bath or Ashford, their present home. Too bold, that was it. She favored her papa in mind and manners. Blunt, assertive, always ready to push you aside and take hold of the reins herself.

Mrs. Hermitage's mind wandered vaguely over her recent domiciles and the impossibility of finding a place to live that was both cheap and pleasant. She had realized that she must remove from expensive London when Herbie died. They went first to a lavish seaside home in Brighton whose rent and requirement for servants were no less than the London abode. This was followed by a move to the less expensive Bath, but even in Bath she managed to run through three thousand in one year. The next stop was Kent, where she could not seem to hobble along on less than twenty-five hundred. She cut every corner known to geometry, but still the annual expenses outran the ever-diminishing interest and they were living on their capital.

Mrs. Hermitage now had fifteen thousand and was in no immediate trouble, but there lurked the knowledge that at some future date they would find themselves living on nothing a year. To avoid this awful fate, she spent like a drunken sailor, outfitting her two hopes for the future in the height of fashion. The girls knew she worried about money, but Papa always used to scold her about her spend-

3

ing, and the daughters had no idea that what they were spending was their future security.

That Sally, the elder, had reached a ripe one and twenty without a suitable offer was a little frightening, but Mama's real hopes were pinned on Melanie. Lord Derwent, come to visit his cousins the Colchesters, had no sooner set an eye on her blond curls and sweet smile than he had extended his week-long visit to a month and spent the better part of it sitting in the Hermitage saloon, mooning over her. He was on the verge of an offer; there was not a doubt in the world of it, and it had been revealed to the mother just moments ago why the offer had taken so long, if four weeks could be considered long in such a matter.

"He requires his guardian's approval before offering, for he is a minor. Not below twenty-one—he is twenty-three—but according to the terms of his father's will, till his twenty-fifth birthday his money is doled out by his uncle, and he is now seeking that gentleman's approval. Without it he could not afford to run a proper household."

The name Monstuart, already half hated by the eager family, was often on Derwent's lips. He called him Monty on those rare occasions when the guardian proved biddable, and Lord Monstuart when he was out of sorts.

"There is no reason why Lord Monstuart should withhold his approval," Sally said. "Melanie is well bred, and we are not precisely paupers."

Mrs. Hermitage pursed her lips and let her daughter dream on. If Sal had the faintest idea how close they were to it, she would institute an unpleasant regime of not buying any clothes, and probably moving into a shabby set of rooms somewhere.

"It seems Monstuart favors a second cousin, Lady Mary DeBeirs."

"How long has he had Lady Mary in his eye for Derwent? Is it a long-standing attachment?"

"Derwent didn't say, dear."

Sally raised her eyes ceilingward in frustration. "Don't you think we should find out?"

Her mother began tut-tutting and saying it seemed a shame to interrupt them; they looked so very happy.

"If we're living in a fool's paradise, let us learn it now," Sally retorted, and went to the grate to pose her question to Derwent. "How long has Monstuart had in mind for you to offer for Lady Mary?" she asked bluntly.

"Oh, lord, since the egg," Derwent told her, smiling placidly. He was a happy man. A slight frown occasionally caused a pleat between his eyes, but it was so infrequent that it had not yet left its calling card. He was fair-haired and blue-eyed, a well-set-up gentleman whom Sally secretly considered a fop. To her sister, however, she never uttered a word of disparagement. Melanie adored him, and for her sake Sally was determined to be at peace with him.

It had occurred to her early in the romance that Derwent and Melanie would be living in London, Lord Monstuart willing, and Sally foresaw some very agreeable visits to their domicile. Ashford bored her. She had not been formally presented in London, but she had attended some informal parties, the theater, and the opera. Fashionable drives through Hyde Park in the afternoon were well remembered, as were some interesting dinner parties at home, where she had been allowed to sit at the table since she was sixteen.

Even at that immature age she had possessed a great deal of conversation and countenance and had been a favorite of the gentlemen If only she could attach someone like Derwent . . . But not *too* much like him, of course. Better an existence in Kent with the prospect of eventually getting to London with a gentleman she could respect than to get to London by marrying a silly fop, just for the change of venue, to use Papa's word.

Sally privately acknowledged that she was getting on in years, but her looks had not yet begun to deteriorate. In fact, they had reached their peak, and it was exigent that Mellie marry Derwent, go to London with him, and invite Sally for a visit. Her interest in forwarding the match was not solely nor even mostly selfish. Melanie was in love, as she reiterated twenty times a day. To hear that Lord Monstuart had had a different alliance in mind for Derwent for some twenty-odd years was not encouraging news.

"Has there been an actual understanding between you and Lady Mary?" she asked Derwent.

"Nothing of the sort. In fact, Monty said himself when we were there at Christmas that I ought to wait a couple of years before offering for her."

"What did you say?" Sally inquired.

"I agreed with him. Absolutely. I wasn't at all eager to have her."

"It's a pity you didn't *say* so, instead of intimating you would offer in a few years." The three conspirators exchanged a speaking glance. Derwent ran tame enough in the house that he knew what a burden Sally Hermitage was to her family. "What was she like?" Sally demanded.

"She's nothing out of the ordinary, I promise you, Miss Hermitage," he said with a warm eye at her extraordinary sister. "It was only her fortune that Monty had his eye on for me."

"An heiress, is she?" Mrs. Hermitage asked with a falling heart. Not a pound of dowry could she see her way clear to granting Mellie. Her present interest was only seven hundred and fifty a year, and to give Mellie money would diminish it to a dangerously low level.

It did not escape Sally's sharp eyes that her mother was incommoded by the news, and she made a mental note to discover the exact sum of their dowries. No offer had been received thus far, and no firm sum had been mentioned recently, but Papa used to speak of ten thousand each. No doubt Lord Montstuart would wish a greater heiress, but Derwent was well to grass. Monstuart might also prefer Lady Mary's title to plain Miss Melanie. Papa had chosen to enter a profession, but both his and his wife's families were more than genteel.

"Thirty thousand is the sum bruited about," Derwent told them.

"Oh, dear." I expected such a sum is very loudly bruited," Mrs. Hermitage declared.

"Not in the least," Derwent told her. "Monty said not to mention it to a soul, or the world would be at her doorstep."

Given such a crafty and money-grubbing guardian as this to contend with, Mrs. Hermitage fell into a fit of the dismals and began calculating how she could do without a few thousand of her meager savings.

"Money has nothing to say about it," Derwent went on cheerfully. "Of course, Lord Monstuart will cut up a little stiff. I expect that, but the fact of the matter is in two years' time I shall be my own man, and he can't stop me from marrying Mellie. Why, I could marry her today and he couldn't stop me— only my money. We can live on her dowry for two years if it comes to that. Naturally I would repay every sou, absolutely," he assured her.

Melanie had no fault to find with this scheme, but it was clear as a pikestaff to Sally that her mother was gasping in discomfort. "When does Lord Monstuart come?" Sally asked.

"I wrote him two weeks ago and have had an answer today. He will come as soon as he can get away. He took a little time to answer, as he was at a houseparty and could not like to leave."

The whole family felt it was the mark of a negligent guardian to put his own pleasure before his charge's welfare, and Sally was immensely relieved. A hint of her feelings put Derwent on the defensive.

"He'll come. Never doubt it. He sometimes takes a little while to come and see my . . ." He fell into a confused silence but soon continued. "The thing is he thinks my infatuation will pass, likely."

Melanie looked at him in wrath, but her wrath was not for her lover, who apparently had more than once applied to his guardian to come and look over a likely bride. No, her wrath was for this tardy guardian, and she gave vent to it in no uncertain terms.

"He'll soon be here. He is at Beauwood, you see. That is the problem," Derwent explained.

"Is it far away?" Mrs. Hermitage asked.

"Lord no, not above fifty or so miles, but he's with Lady Dennison and her Whiggish set and won't want to leave."

"Who is Lady Dennison?" Melanie asked.

"She's his—" The lover fell silent again, wondering how to intimate to an angel the exact nature of his guardian, who was off carousing with his latest flirt. "His friend," Derwent finished limply.

Melanie had no idea what was meant by the umbrella word. "It seems to me you ought to be more to him than a friend," she said, pouting.

"Well, there's politics involved in it, too. It's only Whigs who go to Beauwood. But you're right, of course, absolutely. He never puts my interests first."

Derwent's *absolutelys* were one of the most maddening things about him. They were not uttered with any sense of conviction. They seemed to mean something more like *perhaps*.

Sally looked at her sister askance as her opinion of Lord Monstuart plunged to new depths. This match was coming to look more unlikely by the moment. A suitor whose infatuation promised to be short-lived, a guardian cunning enough to know it and whose own character was such that he wanted the boy to wed an heiress—all this promised little chance of success. Throw in a flirt to detain Monstuart for any length of time, and where were they? Then, too, there was the disquieting doubt engen-

9

dered by Mama's reaction to the mention of dowry. All in all, Sally was eager for Derwent to leave so she could question her mother.

He stayed for his usual interminable visit, and it was not for some time that the desired conversation took place. Mrs. Hermitage, who always liked smooth waters, brushed Sally's inquiries off. But when Melanie decided to retire early, Sally returned to the attack.

"I cannot like this, Mama. If Monstuart doesn't come soon, Derwent will tire of waiting and shab off on us."

"I must own, Sal, I am not at all eager for his arrival. So unpleasant."

"Yes, he sounds a wretch, but he must be dealt with, and the sooner the better. What is the maximum dowry you can see your way clear to giving Mellie?"

Mrs. Hermitage fanned herself with a magazine and said vaguely, "I cannot hope to match Lady Mary DeBeirs's thirty thousand pounds."

"I didn't suppose you could. We are not nabobs, after all, but how much? I think ten thousand would suffice."

Mrs. Hermitage's stout frame gave a little leap. "Ten thousand! Oh, my dear Sal, it is impossible."

Sally looked taken aback. "It was the sum Papa used to mention, but we have fallen on leaner times. How much—"

"Not nearly ten thousand, I fear," her mother said evasively.

"Well, what? Seven thousand, five—*tell* me, Mama."

"I might manage to squeeze out a thousand," her mama said uncertainly.

"A thousand? You joke. Surely you joke. A thousand pounds is nothing. To a man like Derwent it would be an insult."

"Well, it is no joke to me, my dear. I am not at all sure I can afford it."

Sally stared in rising consternation. "What happened to all our money? We were used to be well off. Why, we still are. Look at this house, this saloon, with everything of the first stare. Our clothing alone must cost us . . . Mama, how poor are we?" Sally asked, horrified as her mother's working face presaged very bad news indeed.

"We have nearly fifteen thousand left," she replied, getting the whole over with in one awful declaration.

"*Nearly* fifteen thousand! You mean we are living on seven fifty a year? It is impossible. We spend that on our backs."

"I know, my dear. Everything is shockingly dear, and that is why it will be so difficult to give Mellie any dot."

"But what of all our capital? You cannot mean we have been dipping into that!"

"How else should we live? Of course we are. I am not a magician."

Sally sat dazed, unable to assimilate the situation. "What of the property Papa had in Devon?"

"It brought three thousand, and that was all spent up immediately after his death, when it was sold. The funeral, you recall, and all the crape we had to buy, and the remove to Brighton . . ."

"Were there not other landed assets? No stocks or bonds, nothing?"

"We have our bits of jewelry."

Sally's ivory complexion faded to white. "We are paupers, and here we have been living like kings! How did you come to do such a shatter-brained thing? We should have been living in a rented apartment and saving every penny we could."

Mrs. Hermitage looked and saw the reincarnation of her husband staring at her from those wrathful green eyes. She answered cajolingly. "But my dear, had we done that, Mellie would never have been presented to Derwent. Depend upon it. It is of the utmost importance to keep up a good front when you are in the suds."

"Oh, Mama, that is nonsense and you know it! We could have gone to live with any of our relatives. Uncle Calvin asked us, and Aunt Stepney."

Mrs. Hermitage shivered gently in revulsion. "Uncle Calvin lives in Wales, Sal. One does not live in Wales. And Aunt Stepney is a nip-cheese. You would have met no one, and we would have been underfoot, poor relations."

"Richer relations than we are now."

"Yes, love, but not nearly so well off—in other ways than money, I mean."

Sally sat silent, reeling from the shock of these revelations. She alone of the family had some of the Hermit's sagacity and quick-wittedness and was soon worrying about the real problem. Not Melanie's dowry and not Lord Derwent, but how they should proceed on seven hundred and fifty pounds per annum.

"We must move to smaller quarters and be rid of

some of these servants and carriages. Fortunately we have enough clothing to last years."

"I knew you would say that. That is exactly why I didn't like to tell you."

"Yes, because you knew you were wrong to squander our life savings, Mama."

"We shall retrench after we get Melanie bounced off. You and I might be comfortable in smaller quarters, for no one of any importance will bother with you—*us*! But with Lord Monstuart coming, we must keep up a good appearance."

"He is not coming to inspect our home, Mama, but to see how heavily you are willing to come down to nab Derwent for Mellie. I think we might as well consider Derwent lost and—"

"Oh, Sal! How unfeeling—you know Mellie's dear heart is set on him."

"Yes, and his on her, for the next day or two. But when Monstuart arrives, he will scotch the plan."

"He shan't!" Mrs. Hermitage said with unusual vehemence. "If necessary we can do as Derwent says and live on our capital till he comes into his own."

"He had no notion how poor we are when he said that. He wouldn't take our life savings, yours and mine as well as Mellie's. I would have a very poor notion of him if he did."

"He would repay every sou; he said so."

"Yes, repay it to his wife—to himself, in other words. He was speaking of *Melanie's* dowry. He didn't know the true situation. When he learns it, he'll renege."

Mrs. Hermitage heaved a sigh of vexation but refused to be utterly despondent. "We have not met

13

Monstuart yet. Let us wait and see what sort of gentleman he is. He might be very biddable. There is no saying."

"He is as cunning as may be. He cannot be a sentimental man or he would have come at once when he received Derwent's message. I even wonder about his morals. This Lady Dennison is obviously someone's wife."

"She might be a widow—or his fiancée."

"Yes, if her husband left her well to grass. I wonder he doesn't angle for Lady Mary himself."

"Why, he would be too old for her. Derwent is twenty-three, and Monstuart is his uncle. He will be forty or fifty."

"And a rake into the bargain. A hardheaded man who considers marriage a business transaction, and love a game to be played on the side."

"I don't know where you get such ideas, Sally. I'm sure you are sophisticated beyond your years. It is exactly the sort of speech that put all men off at Bath."

"I had that much sophistication before ever I left London. I do have eyes in my head, you know, and saw very well what was going on among your friends."

Mrs. Hermitage's fine eyes flashed blue fire. "If you are referring to Samantha Barnow, I will have you know she and your papa were just friends."

"Yes, Mama, as Lord Monstuart and Lady Dennison are just friends. I am not seven years old; you don't have to hide from me that Papa was a shocking flirt. Well, you had a few beaux calling in the afternoon yourself when Papa was at work. I seem to remember a Sir Darrow somebody or other drop-

14

ping in with suspicious regularity, but never mind. I am neither judge nor jury. Perhaps there is some sense in what you say. Monstuart will be calling eventually, I trust, and till he leaves we shan't bother trying to cut back. But as soon as he's gone, whether the match with Derwent comes off or not, we must curtail our spending and hang on to what we can of that paltry fifteen thousand pounds."

"Certainly we must, my dear. And I have just had a delightful notion. If Monstuart is fifty or so, as we think, I might make a few eyes at him and see if my fading charms have still sufficient strength to woo him."

"As they woo Mr. Heppleworth, eh, Mama?" Sally smiled.

Mrs. Hermitage was forty, and a very stylish, well-preserved forty that might pass for a few years less. What white hair she had was well concealed by her blond curls. Time's ravages to her complexion were hidden by a judicious use of the rouge pot. It was often discussed *en famille* that Mr. Heppleworth was infatuated with her. Mama had an inkling it was Sally he came to see, using herself as an excuse. A balding gentleman of forty-five would not like to make a complete cake of himself in front of his friends.

Sally fell silent, considering if her mother might be induced to have Heppleworth. He was a country gentleman, but a well-greased one, and would solve their money problems very tidily. She was a clever girl, but from considering Mr. Heppleworth an old man, she had never thought of his friendliness to her in any light other than avuncular. Many of her

15

father's old friends had flirted with her in the same gallant fashion.

"We shall see," Mrs. Hermitage said. "If Monstuart doesn't care for me, you can roll your eyes at him, Sal."

Miss Hermitage had already decided Monstuart was a rake and a libertine. She had no intention of encouraging his advances. "I'm not that eager for Mellie's marriage."

"How about your own? You cannot be happy to see little Mellie beating you to the altar. And Monstuart is very wealthy, Derwent says."

Sally considered the matter a moment. "Well, as you say, if he proves biddable . . ."

Chapter Two

The Hermitages were not long in doubt as to what sort of a gentleman Lord Monstuart was. He landed in on them the next morning at an inconvenient ten-thirty, when they were not accustomed to receiving Derwent till eleven. When Monstuart arrived with his nephew, it was only Miss Hermitage who was up and ready to receive a caller. Mama was adding the coup de grace to Mellie's blond crown in the shape of a blue bow, to match her eyes. It chanced that Sally was just sweeping down the curved staircase as the butler admitted the callers.

She surmised on the instant who the tall, severe-faced gentleman with Derwent must be, and was happy she had put on a fashionable gown of green sarcenet that set off her dark hair and ivory complexion to great advantage, for Lord Monstuart was obviously from the tip of the ton. He wore his dark hair in the Brutus style, with a dark blue coat of superfine that bespoke the tailoring of Weston. His meticulously tied cravat was done in the Oriental style. A curled beaver, a malacca walking stick, and

York tan gloves were being handed to Rinkin as she came down.

Sally was aware of a close scrutiny from a pair of cold gray eyes, accompanied by a surprised lift of two slashes of black eyebrows. An aquiline nose and a square jaw lent distinction to a face that was interesting rather than handsome. Too young for Mama to wind 'round her finger, she thought, and too wicked for me. She was almost frightened by his forbidding aspect, but familiarity with society allowed her to make the pair welcome with none of the discomposure she was feeling.

She asked Rinkin to inform Mama the gentlemen had arrived, and ushered them into the Rose Saloon. It was a room much admired in Ashford. The Hermit had not stinted in his furnishings, and Mama had not skimped in having the walls painted an ivory white, with gilt trim on the decorative medallions. It was a feminine room, with a rose-patterned carpet, rose velvet hangings at the windows, a fine white marble Adams fireplace, and many expensive bibelots gracing delicate tables and wall brackets.

Monstuart's slate eyes flickered over it, showing no approval nor again any approval when they settled once more on Miss Hermitage. Still, that he did not show disapproval was felt to be a wonder to the young lady. There was some superciliousness in those brows, still raised at a questioning angle, and the lips, which refused to raise a fraction at the ends when introductions were made. Sally took a chair and set herself to the task of amusing the guests till her family came down.

She essayed a few comments to Lord Monstuart,

who replied monosyllabically, with still that surprised look on his saturnine face. She soon found herself put off by his manner and turned to Derwent. "Mellie will be down presently," she assured him.

"There is no hurry, Miss Hermitage," Monstuart said. "We are happy for the opportunity to have a few words alone with you."

She blinked her eyes at such a strange statement, but it was Derwent who made sense of it. "It ain't Miss Hermitage I'm—that is, it's Mellie you've come to see."

Monstuart's steely eyes froze a moment on Sally, till she felt her bones were turning to ice. It was an extraordinarily peculiar look, partly of surprise, but there was an assessing quality to it, too, as though he had slid her under a microscope for minute examination.

"Ah, forgive me. I was told I was to meet a beautiful young lady, and as I have done so, I fell into the error of thinking you were Derwent's intended," he explained. Sally felt no pleasure at the compliment.

"Told you she was a blonde," Derwent reminded him.

"So you did. I ought to have known it in any case, n'est-ce pas?" His eyes returned to Sally. "My nephew has an unswerving propensity in that direction."

She noticed the startled expression was gone from his face. The eyebrows had settled down to a more normal angle, but the new arrangement of features was not more pleasing. He had assumed a sardonic smile. Now what is so amusing? Sally found herself wondering. He had been amazed that Derwent had chosen *her*—that's what it was! She was naturally not flattered with this interpretation. That she would never in a million years have chosen Derwent was not considered. It was an insult for the uncle to think he would not have chosen her.

Monstuart was further surprised to see a flash of anger from the feline emerald eyes regarding him. He looked closely, wondering at the reason for it, but before he had time to consider it, the other ladies were in and being introduced. As soon as he saw Melanie, he knew it was she and no other Derwent would have chosen. A vastly beautiful blond doll, with a soft shy smile and pretty manners.

He was relieved that the whole family turned out in such high style and lived amid such opulence. To have let Derwent off the leash had been a foolish thing to do. Naturally he would be fancying himself in love, and it was kind of Fate to have cast such a respectable young lady in his path. Lady Mary's plain appearance didn't stand a chance against this porcelain doll. He unbent somewhat from his first stiffness, enough to make a few polite comments to Mrs. Hermitage and his nephew's choice. His errand was to look over the prospective bride; she passed muster within minutes, so far as appearance and behavior were concerned. From then onward, Monstuart's gaze more often than not was on the sleek, raven-haired enchantress. He noticed that hers strayed frequently to him as well. She sat so still she might have been made of stone, but stone was not the material her supple body suggested. More like a jungle cat hiding to pounce on its prey.

It was unusual to find so elegant a creature in

the country. Her hair, her gown, her manner—all had the aura of the city. From the corner of his eye, he observed her in three-quarter profile. From that angle a long sweep of black lashes projected, while her high cheekbone gave some indication of the face's shape. Studying her in this surreptitious manner, Monstuart knew he had not seen such an Incomparable in several seasons. He was keenly interested in Incomparables. When he directed some inconsequential remark to Sally, she turned to face him, answering with a smile.

Her teeth were white and rounded at the corners in an unusual and attractive way. There wasn't a sharp angle anywhere in her whole makeup. She was a delightful bundle of supple curves. Like Derwent first casting eyes on Melanie, Monstuart decided on the spot he would make a visit of indeterminate duration with his relations the Colchesters.

When the butler brought wine, it was Miss Hermitage who handed Monstuart his glass. He looked at her long-fingered, graceful hand, with a fine but small emerald ring on one finger, and observed her delicate pink nails, carefully manicured. He hadn't seen such fastidious grooming on any woman outside of the muslin company, whose bodies were their only asset. When tasted, the wine to be proved unexceptional. Monstuart was so favorably impressed that the image of Lady Mary Debeirs began to recede from the forefront of his mind.

From the moonstruck expression on Derwent's face, Monstuart saw little likelihood of detaching him from Miss Melanie. It would be a relief to have the lad settled down. He was demmed tired of pulling on his leash. He had no real authority over anything but the purse strings, and even that minimal control was dwindling as Derwent approached his majority. The rest of the visit would be mere formality. The dowry wouldn't match DeBeirs's, of course, but the Hermitages seemed a suitable connection. He turned purposefully to Mrs. Hermitage. "Shall we leave the youngsters and get the business settled, ma'am?"

Mrs. Hermitage cast an appealing glance on her elder daughter, who returned a look of sympathy but had no concrete help to offer. The words "lamb to the slaughter" popped into Sally's head. With her insides shaking like a blancmange, Mrs. Hermitage led Lord Monstuart to the study. The closing of the door sounded dreadfully like a death knell.

Sally remained behind with the others. It was never pleasant being with the lovers. They ignored one totally and sat staring at each other and smiling, but today it was sheer hell. Sally's mind was in the study with her mother and Monstuart. What would he say upon learning that there was not a penny of dowry? She found his character impossible to gauge. He appeared a cold person from the little she had seen; calculating, looking for a flaw. Yet he had expressed no open disapproval.

The meeting in the study was brief, but it was the most enervating quarter hour of Mrs. Hermitage's life. Her husband's rages at her extravagance were nothing to it, and his temper had always sent her into a swoon. She was completely floored by the pair of steel-gray eyes staring at her as though she were a lunatic when she opened her budget to him.

"A thousand pounds! *A thousand pounds!*" he exclaimed in disbelief. "If this is a joke, it isn't funny. If you're serious, madam, it's a demmed good joke." But her pink face told him it was no joke.

When Sally heard the study door open, she could no longer hold her seat. She bolted into the hall to see her mother on the point of tears, her face fallen and her eyes anguished. Behind Monstuart's back, she shook her head and threw up her hands in despair. Monstuart was striding at an angry pace toward the saloon, and upon intercepting Sally, he said coldly, "Tell my nephew to come now, please."

His imperious manner sent her blood racing. "What has happened?" Sally demanded.

He turned a sneering face to her. "Negotiations have broken down. I was called here on a fool's errand, as you have nothing with which to negotiate."

Sally's hands clenched into fists, and her lungs felt suffocated. Looking to the study, she saw her mother go back into the room, shoulders sagging. Her anger rose to see her so overwrought. "You have not forbidden the match out of hand!"

"I have forbidden it to prevent being out of pocket."

"It won't be *your* pocket!"

"No, and it won't be my nephew's either. Try another quarry, miss. You'll find the bird you've chosen is not so easily plucked."

"No one is trying to take advantage of him. He is in love."

"He is 'in love' with one pretty face or another fifty times a year. He doesn't marry them, however."

23

"No, you mean to see him marry Lady Mary DeBeirs's thirty thousand pounds, whether he likes her or not, and take care that no one else finds out about her fortune."

Monstuart's eyes diminished to slivers of ice. "You are well informed. She's one of the ladies I have in mind, but whether he eventually marries her or someone else, you may be sure the Earl of Derwent will not marry a solicitor's undowered daughter."

He stalked to the doorway of the Rose Saloon, where some little hint of the altercation had already been overheard. Melanie and Derwent were standing, staring at each other in dismay.

"Come along, Derwent," Monstuart said in the tone a schoolmaster might use to an unruly ten-year-old.

"I usually stay awhile," Derwent was so bold as to mention, but in a tentative voice.

"Come!" The monosyllable sounded like the bark of an angry dog. With a last, languishing look at Melanie, Derwent went.

The three ladies immediately converged in the Rose Saloon. Melanie was weeping noisily. Mrs. Hermitage was not far from it, and Sally was foaming with fury. The reason for the match being disallowed was difficult for Melanie to comprehend.

"But why won't you give me any money?" she demanded in a tone of pique, with an accusing look at her mother.

"Because we don't have any," Sally said with a snort.

"But Derwent is rich," the girl replied in confusion.

24

"He will be richer when he marries; you may be sure of that," Sally informed her sniveling sister.

"I never had such a wretched experience in my life," Mrs. Hermitage said weakly, and sank, puffing onto a petit point chair.

Sally's heart constricted with pity, but her voice was hard. "What did he say?" she demanded.

"My dear, he as well as accused us of being fortune hunters, or worse. To speak of my having set up a velvet trap, bated with two ..." Words failed her, and like her younger daughter, she was soon weeping into a handkerchief.

Angry green sparks flashed in Sally's eyes. "Two what?"

"Two well-plumed chicks," Mrs. Hermitage gasped, and bawled harder.

Sally turned to the window. If the gentlemen had not already been on their way down the street, she would have run after them and banged their heads together. She was nearly as angry with Derwent as Monstuart. Most of all, she was angry that Monstuart's insults contained a grain of truth. What *were* they doing but setting up an establishment well beyond their means, in the hope of trapping rich husbands? That both she and Mellie had been unaware of it salved her conscience somewhat, but it did not calm her nerves or lessen her anger one iota.

"I wonder you didn't scratch his eyes out," she said.

"Oh, my dear, and that is not the worst of it," her mother continued. "He thinks you and I and all our relatives intend to batten ourselves on Derwent. 'A set of dirty dishes,' he called us. As though

25

your Uncle Calvin or Aunt Stepney would *think* of such a thing. You and I are the worst of the lot in that respect."

"I hope you didn't tell him that!"

"I don't know what I may have said. You have often mentioned visiting them in London, but I never agreed you planned to batten yourself on them permanently. One thing I did set him straight on is that we are not *dirty*, for I had that nice liver-shaped bathtub put in just last year."

Sally gave a snide grimace. "What had he to say to that?"

"The man is unconscionable. He said the likes of us had best keep our feathers plumed, for it is all we have to offer. I swear, Sal, I think he meant—something—not quite nice."

Sally's mouth fell open in shock. A cold anger gripped her, rendering her speechless.

"I hate him! I hate him!" Melanie declared, raising her tear-streaked face from her lap. She had never been heard to express hatred for a soul in her life before. Even a convicted murderer was allowed to have been under great strain, and the French couldn't help being Frenchmen.

Seeing that some order must be brought from the chaos around them, Sally said, "This is getting us nowhere. He has forbidden the match, but we had foreseen that possibility. It does not mean no match will take place. Derwent has already suggested living on our money for the two years till he comes into his own."

Mrs. Hermitage peered hopefully at her elder daughter. "You said it wouldn't do," she reminded her.

"That was before I met Monstuart. What better can he expect from lightskirts? I begin to think the threat of it will do very well—for a lever to force him into accepting the match."

"He'll never accept anything," Mrs. Hermitage predicted gloomily.

"Will he not? He may hold the cheese, but the knife is in Derwent's hands. When he comes back . . ."

"He didn't say he'd come back," Melanie said, and fell into a fresh bout of tears at his lapse. Derwent always said he would come back.

"I don't suppose he means to leave the neighborhood without saying good-bye to us," Sally pointed out. Her eyes narrowed to green slits, and her nostrils quivered dangerously. Watching her, Mrs. Hermitage felt a shiver up her spine. Sal had hardly a feature in common with her father, but in this mood, she bore such an uncanny resemblance that Mrs. Hermitage was strongly of a mind to let Sal take the reins.

"When he comes, we shall trip the spring in our velvet trap. You must plume yourself well, sister," Sally said in a voice of silken menace.

"Monstuart won't let him come," Melanie hiccoughed. "He had the coldest eyes, like an iceberg."

A sinking sensation came over Sally. Melanie was a simpleton, but she was right about this. Derwent had risen like a puppet on a string at a command from his guardian. It was incomprehensible to her that a man of independent means should be so subservient. The matter was discussed for a long time, but all depended on Derwent's coming, and

27

in the end there was nothing to do but wait and see if he came.

To do Lord Derwent justice, he intended not only to return but to proceed with the match in the teeth of his uncle's strenuous objections. He knew he was slipping deep into sin to set up his back against Monstuart, who had directed his life for fifteen years as a substitute father, but he intended to do it all the same.

Though he had been in love numberless times, he had never been so deeply, hopelessly, irrevocably in love as now. The string of blondes who had preceded Mellie were but weak imitations of her. She was the apotheosis of his dream. The sweetest, blondest, most adorable girl in the world. He hadn't a doubt he would die if deprived of her. Nothing of this was said to his uncle, however. Derwent's courage was not so great that he intended a direct confrontation. He would slip away as soon as he could escape from Monstuart, and marry behind his back.

When Lord Monstuart returned to the Colchesters, he was in a foul mood. He gave his hostess a hint that she had been negligent to have let Derwent fall into the clutches of a fortune-hunting bunch of harpies. His cousin stared at him in shocked disbelief.

"The Hermitages are unexceptionable, Monstuart," she said at once.

"No, ma'am, they only appear unexceptionable, and hardly that, with the late Mr. Hermitage a mere solicitor."

"Oh, but not just any solicitor. He was the Hermit."

Monstuart, usually a highly composed gentleman, gave a start of alarm and exclaimed, "What?" in a loud voice.

"He was the Hermit. You must have heard of him—he was famous."

"Certainly I knew the Hermit, but he was as rich as may be. His widow and family would not be living off their capital in some provincial backwater."

Mrs. Colchester stiffened at this slur on her chosen neighborhood. "Some of us like it here," she informed him.

"You said these people come from Bath."

"They were at Bath for a while, and Brighton, too, before settling here."

"I thought I had heard the family moved to Bath. They ought to be wealthy."

"I made sure they were. Everything is of the first style of elegance. You never mean their pockets are to let!" she inquired with avid curiosity and not a little satisfaction. Mrs. Hermitage's exquisite toilette had plagued her for many months.

"Not completely broke," Monstuart admitted, "but in tighter straits than the Hermit's family ought to be. They are related to any number of good families that should . . . Oh, lord!" Monstuart realized that his quick temper had led him into a highly disagreeable situation, antagonizing so many worthies. He was often called upon to rescue Derwent from such persons as he imagined the Hermitages to be, and wasted no ceremony in the doing of it. Perhaps his reaction on this occasion had been a little more ferocious than usual.

In some danger from the feline lady himself, he had intended making the rupture totally irreparable, to forestall any unseemly alliance on his own part. Demands as to why he had not been informed of the family's background were futile. He hadn't, and he had acted unconscionably as a result. He still didn't consider the match with Miss Melanie a good one by any manner of means, but the extrication must be more seemly than he had made it.

He must go back and try to smooth the many ruffled feathers he had raised in that velvet roost. He wished to keep Derwent away from them, however, and so gave no indication of his plan. He took the boy out in the country that afternoon to try to talk some sense into him. The silence that greeted his every word was not the silent acquiescence usually encountered. There was a sullen set about Derwent's lips that promised trouble. And really he couldn't do a demmed thing about it but give him a good Bear Garden jaw, which he did.

The boy did not openly oppose him, so the objections to the match were only raised, condemned as intolerable, and then the talk turned to what Monstuart considered more cheerful subjects, such as Lady Mary DeBeirs. "We'll stay here a day or two with the Colchesters, then take a run up to Chêne Baie," He said bracingly. Chêne Baie, was the abode of the DeBeirses. There was Norman blood in the family, and French names aplenty. Unfortunately there wasn't an iota of beauty or charm in a cartload of them. Derwent sat sulky and silent throughout the trip.

In the evening, Monstuart excused himself on the pretext of visiting other relatives in the neighborhood. Derwent saw an excellent chance to nip back to Mellie and assure her he had not been discouraged from marrying her. He felt quite manly at his

30

prospective future, flying in the face of Monty's authority, taking on the care of a penniless wife and her family.

To fool Derwent, Monstuart turned his team west upon leaving the Colchesters, planning to approach the Hermitage residence circuitously. Deceived, for he never suspected a trick, Derwent set out by the more direct route as soon as his uncle was down the road, and got there before him.

Chapter Three

There was considerable elevation in the spirits of the Hermitage ladies when Lord Derwent was shown into their Rose Saloon that evening. Hopes had not been high that he would dare to oppose his imperious uncle. The four were in the sort of mood generated by a successful bucking of authority, made merrier by the element of romance that pervaded the room. Derwent stated firmly that he would take care of them all, "absolutely," and Mrs. Hermitage said as firmly that she would help. With fifteen thousand pounds to tide them over till Derwent's fifteen thousand a year became his, the situation did not appear at all desperate.

There perhaps lingered at the back of their minds the dread that Lord Monstuart might have something to say in the matter, but such an unpleasant contingency was not spoken of. The talk was all of a remove to Gravenhurst, Derwent's estate in Dorchester, at his disposal in spite of his uncle.

Sally heard it and frowned. "I thought you planned to go to London!" she exclaimed. That had always been the plan before Monstuart's arrival.

"Monty will be there," Derwent said.

Sally stared at his cowardice. It angered her that Monstuart should have anything to say in leading their lives. "What of it? Are you afraid of him? You must present Melanie to society, Derwent. Why, it would look as though you were ashamed of her if you whisked her off to Gravenhurst." Melanie, who did not share her sister's love of high society, looked an accusing question at her hero.

"You're right, Sally, absolutely," Derwent said at once. "We shall go to London for the Season first." Really, the boy was criminally easy to lead.

With such interesting goings-on to distract them, the ladies didn't hear the front knocker. When Lord Monstuart was shown into the Rose Saloon, he was faced with the highly unpleasant sight of his cocker of a nephew being fawned upon by three laughing ladies, making him feel, no doubt, like a monarch. Monstuart assumed this was the way they had beguiled the boy, by dancing attendance on him, feeding him wine and compliments. His brow lowered, his nostrils quivered, and an angry liverish hue suffused his face. It was thus that he appeared to the four when his presence was noted. A pall of silence immediately fell over the noisy room, as if the schoolmaster had come into the class and caught his students out in some ribaldry.

"Uncle!" Derwent exclaimed, jumping to his feet with a guilty start.

"Ladies, Derwent," Monstuart said in a thin voice as he nodded his head and stepped in. His impulse was to take his nephew by the scruff of the neck and drag him by main force from the room and the neighborhood, but he quickly squashed the impulse.

"You said you were going to call on the Gibbards!" Derwent said. His pink face told them all that he had sneaked off behind his uncle's back, and he had been bragging about how he had not knuckled under to Monstuart.

"They were not at home," Monstuart replied in glacial accents.

"What in the deuce made you come *here*?" Derwent asked.

Sally, sizing up the situation, rose and in three smooth strides was at Monstuart's side, a brilliant glitter in her eyes, and on her lips a small smile of triumph. She curtsied and said primly, "We are honored that we should be second choice for your visit, milord. Do come in. You will think us uncivil, but you must not think we are unhappy to see Derwent's uncle. Pray, be seated."

"Thank you," he replied, and followed her to a chair at the edge of the erstwhile happy group, throwing a measured look to his nephew. Derwent flinched visibly and fell silent.

The new arrival was punctiliously offered a glass of wine and a biscuit by Miss Hermitage. He accepted both with a coolly polite "thank you." After this effort at civility, an appalling silence fell over the group.

Monstuart, after finishing his biscuit, broke the silence. "You didn't mention you were coming here this evening, Derwent. I am happy you're here, however. No doubt you have come, like me, to take your leave of the ladies."

Derwent looked to Melanie and smiled a smile as

reassuring as he dared to make under his uncle's awful stare. He answered not a word.

It was Miss Hermitage who was pushed into speech by an appealing glance from her allies. "It is not Lord Derwent's intention to leave us quite so soon, milord. We have some considerable matters to discuss."

"Indeed?" Monstuart had come to conciliate and was not to be goaded to more savagery by this taunting beauty. He turned deliberately to Mrs. Hermitage. "I was not aware, when we spoke this morning, ma'am, that your late husband was the Hermit, if I may use his nickname."

"Certainly you may. Everyone called him that," the widow said, happy to see no immediate ruffling of the waters. "Because of the name, you know, and not because of any unsocial qualities. Quite the contrary, Herbie was very sociable. We used to know everyone in London."

"You must miss the pleasures of the city."

"We did at first, but we are settling down to country life. Well, town life, which seems like the deep country to us."

"Pity." But if, as he assumed, this retirement was for the purpose of saving money, it must be inefficacious. Everywhere around him, in both decor and dress, there were signs of lavish spending. The family were either fools or schemers; he set himself to the task of discovering which.

"You have managed to create quite an urban nook here in the country," Monstuart said, glancing at the painted walls, the fine pictures and velvet draperies.

"It wasn't easy—or cheap," Mrs. Hermitage replied. "The walls were a hideous mustard color when we hired the places. Made us all look bran-faced."

His dark eyes flickered over the ladies' glowing complexions and he replied, "That must have taken some doing."

"I daresay the dirty windows helped. We have fixed the place up a little, for we were not accustomed to living in squalor. It was very dear," she repined while her elder daughter shot her a quelling frown.

Sally saw that her mother was about to enter on one of her diatribes on the dearness of everything. This had been one of her pet themes since Papa's death. She sincerely wished her mother had gone on to tell her just how ill they could afford all the dear acquisitions.

"Everything is expensive nowadays," he said leadingly.

"Expensive? It's shocking! Why, to have that very chair you are sitting in covered cost me five guineas, and Melanie worked the embroidered covering with her own fingers."

"Melanie is an excellent needlewoman," Derwent tossed in, happy for any detail that enhanced her value.

Monstuart's unenthusiastic "Very nice" could hardly be construed as a compliment, especially as his body covered her handiwork completely and he made no motion of rising to admire it.

The group chatted on for a while, long enough for the marquess to ascertain that the mother was a fool. He acquitted her of conniving to entrap Derwent, but not of being a ninny, and certainly not of promising to be a very poor connection for his nephew. Already he had observed that it was Miss Hermitage who was looked to for guidance by the group. Her character was still to be determined.

At length, Mrs. Hermitage took up her embroidery and settled down to work. Her eyes roamed often to Derwent and Mellie in the corner. "I need a better light," she said, and moved to a chair closer to the lovers, who whispered uneasily between themselves, with many a cautious look toward the enemy interloper.

Monstuart turned his conversation to Miss Hermitage. She regarded him with a smug little smile of satisfaction that he was eager to remove from her face. "And are you quite happy to be away from London, ma'am?" he asked politely.

"The peace and quiet of Ashford just suit me."

"You, too, are an excellent needlewoman, I trust?" He glanced at her idle fingers as he spoke.

"No, I read a good deal, and I enjoy riding."

"Another shockingly expensive pastime."

"Its expense need not concern you."

"The expenses of the whole family concern me, when it is your intention to dump them in Derwent's lap."

A mischievous smile lurked at the corner of Sally's lips. "You are conceding defeat so soon?" she taunted him.

"The word *intention* does not necessarily denote execution, Miss Hermitage. I was merely commenting on your style of life." Monstuart hastened to change the topic when he saw he was slipping into bad manners. It was his hope to indicate that he was still very much against the match, without repeating his former insults. "I think you were unwise to leave London," he said.

"Your opinion must stand for a good deal with us, of course," she answered ironically, "but we are happy here."

"Slim pickings. I seem to recall the Hermit was said to possess the next Season's Incomparable, at the time of his death. You would have done better to remain in London, when you were at a marriageable age," he added. No emphasis stressed the word "marriageable," but the past tense revealed his subtle meaning. "You planned to return when your sister married, no doubt?"

It was the age insult that lent a quick flash of anger to her eyes, but it was the innuendo that she spoke of. "We didn't plan to live with Derwent! Of course, as things stand now, that may be necessary."

"As things stand now that I am here, it is unlikely in the extreme," he countered.

Sally's eyes lifted to observe him from beneath her long lashes. "If you refuse to forward him any of his own money, he must batten himself on us till he reaches his maturity," she retaliated, stressing repetition of his own ill-chosen words.

Monstuart swallowed it in silence, but his temper was rising. "I find it strange you did not choose to live with relatives, as money is so severe a problem with you."

"There is no accounting for taste," she answered demurely.

His eyes roved around the richly appointed saloon. "There is no taste for accounting in this household," he retorted.

38

A little laugh escaped from Miss Hermitage, and he smiled involuntarily in response. "Touché, milord. I did not look for wit in Derwent's guardian."

"So I gather. You judge me by the one specimen of my family to which you have been exposed. Derwent is my sister's son, and the female line of my family, like most," he added with a challenging glance, "is not bright."

Sally felt her blood rise to the challenge. "I am said to favor Papa. He was not considered a dull gentleman."

Monstuart had already begun to confirm who was the brains in the family. "There is some resemblance," he admitted.

"Did you know him?" she asked, startled. "I don't recall seeing you about the house."

"I was never at your father's house, but he was occasionally at mine. He handled a business matter for me some years ago."

"What matter was that?" she asked with sharp interest. Papa's cases were generally in the nature of *causes célèbres*. She had no recollection of reading Lord Monstuart's name in the journals.

"The details escape me," he answered evasively. "It was some years ago. We occasionally met afterward for a game of cards or chess."

"Papa was a great chess player."

"Do you play?"

"Very little."

"The country offers so few entertainments. I wonder if you might be induced to give me a game," he suggested. He looked toward the lovers in the corner, and the mama, and stifled a yawn behind his fingers.

It was Monstuart's intention to remain as long as Derwent, and Miss Hermitage had already guessed as much. She rose to get the board and assemble the pieces. Watching her glide across the room, he found her as admirable a sight from the rear as from any other angle.

Sally began to set up the chessboard, but she had not played in several years and was unsure where to place the various pieces. Holding a carved ivory queen, she let her fingers hover above the squares, catching her lower lip between her teeth. He studied the white hands with the delicate pink nails, then the little rounded white teeth, and said not a word as she put every piece save the pawns in the wrong squares. When the job was done, he rapidly shuffled them around to the conventional positions, without a word.

"I haven't played in an age," she admitted.

"I assumed as much," he replied, but didn't offer to call off the game. She would have preferred conversation, during which she hoped to score him off for calling them ladybirds.

Monstuart started off with a conventional opening; it was the only conventional move made during the game. Miss Hermitage had obviously not the least notion what she was about. Bishops were hopped like knights, knights shoved straight forward or diagonally, and even a pawn was endowed with the power of taking three or four squares at a leap. She was a wretched player, but such an entrancing one to watch that he went on for some minutes without saying a word. He watched her fluttering hands, and her face tensed in willful con-

40

centration as she tried vainly to remember the route her chosen piece should take.

"Tell me," he said a while latter, "are we playing chess, or hopscotch?"

"I think *you* are playing chess and *I* am playing hopscotch," she confessed, "and it is a pity we are playing our separate games on the same board. Truth to tell, I haven't the foggiest notion what I'm doing."

"In that case, you are doing it extremely well. I can't believe the Hermit's daughter is so dull she can't master the moves. Shall I refresh your memory a little? The queen can go . . ." He went on to explain the rudiments.

"It's much too confusing. Let us play piquet instead," Sally suggested, throwing up her hands.

"No, no! You give up too easily. It will be an excellent diversion for you, here in the country, with many a long evening to kill." He glanced at his watch and at his nephew, but there was no sign of Derwent leaving yet, so they continued their confusing game of chess, till at length Monstuart rose and said peremptorily to his nephew that it was getting late.

Derwent felt his uncle was coming around, and with a squeeze of his intended's fingers and a smile that promised future bliss, he was torn away. The three ladies sat around the fire later, asking one another what the second visit from Monstuart augured.

"He was much more civil than he was this morning," Mrs. Hermitage said hopefully. "He apologized for what he said earlier—on the way out, you

41

know, he murmured something to that effect. An apology does not come easily to him."

"He also said he and Derwent had come to take their leave," Sally reminded them.

"Derwent is coming back tomorrow." Melanie smiled.

"If Monstuart lets him," Sally added.

"As to that," Mrs. Hermitage said with a coy look at her elder daughter, "I think you handled him very wisely, Sal."

"I didn't 'handle' him at all. He has no idea of allowing the match, but I don't see how he can prevent it."

"He can't," Mrs. Hermitage said firmly, for Melanie's benefit, but she was by no means convinced of it. On this hopeful note, they went to bed.

Chapter Four

If a second visit from Monstuart led to curiosity, a third on the next morning threw the ladies into alarm. He had come to take his leave. Why, then, had he returned? But return he did, and at no late hour either. As on the day before, the gentlemen arrived at an inconvenient ten-thirty. Melanie always made a prolonged toilette. Next to her visits from Derwent, they were the most enjoyable part of her day.

On this occasion, Miss Hermitage was also unprepared for company, but she was ready sooner than the others, so it was her lot to go belowstairs and entertain the callers till reinforcements arrived. As she glided noiselessly toward the Rose Saloon, she heard Monstuart's deep voice coming from within. He spoke in a lowered tone, but his words were audible. "I think you have chosen poorly," he said. It was enough to get her hackles up. He was trying to talk Derwent out of the match and was ill-bred enough to do it under their own roof!

Her eyes were already flashing and her color was high when she entered the room. The welcome bestowed on Monstuart was a welcome in name only. "Good morning," she said in a voice that would freeze live coals. "How very early you are up and about these days, Derwent," she continued more affably to the younger gentleman. "We are not accustomed to seeing you before eleven."

Lord Derwent was never at his best with Miss Hermitage. "It's a jolly fine day, you know, and I hoped Mellie might come out with me for a drive."

"She will be delighted," Sally replied with just a flicker of a triumphant glance to the guardian. "Have you come to take your leave of us again, Lord Monstuart?" she asked.

"I have decided to prolong my visit."

It was about the worst news he could deliver. He was going to stay on, trying to talk Derwent out of the marriage by reminding him he had "chosen poorly." A sardonic smile thinned his lips. "You conceal your joy remarkably well, ma'am. I congratulate you."

"I doubt you will find much to amuse you in Ashford," she said curtly.

"On the contrary, I find a great deal to amuse me," he countered. There was a little something in his smile that hinted she herself was a source of amusement, as one might take amusement from a raree-show or the antics of a monkey.

"Absolutely," Derwent said eagerly. "Drives and rides and dinner parties and assemblies. There are any number of things to do in Ashford. I never saw such a lively spot, for a dull little country town, you know."

"With chess and embroidery and reading to fill any little interstices that might occur in such a crowded calendar," Monstuart added, leaving the words to convey their own impression of tedium, for there was no sarcasm in his tone.

"We do not hope to match the gaiety of Beauwood," Sally said pointedly, and regarded Monstuart with a meaningful eye.

He refused to take offense but managed to add a little to his reply. "How should you, indeed?"

It was well that the absent Hermitage ladies appeared at that moment. Monstuart received a baleful scowl from Melanie, but Mrs. Hermitage, who still remembered her scold from him, felt he was not a person to be offended and was very civil. She offered wine and a good many expressions of worried delight at his call.

"Will you do me the honor of driving out with me, Miss Hermitage?" Monstuart asked when Derwent and Melanie rose to leave.

Sally was unsure in what manner the gentlemen had arrived. If it was in two open carriages, as the spring weather made possible, her inclination was to remain at home. On the other hand, if Monstuart was to make an unwelcome third in Derwent's carriage, she felt she must go, for her sister's sake. Derwent solicited her company, saying in a transparently pleading way, "I came in Monty's carriage. We will all be as merry as grigs in Uncle's rig together."

Sally saw her duty, and she did it. Monstuart didn't comment on her decision, but she knew by his mocking look that he had engineered the matter of one carriage, done it for the sole purpose of ensuring her presence.

"Where shall we go?" Melanie asked.

Sally thought the best place to go was some spot where they might descend from the carriage to walk, thus giving the young lovers some privacy. With this end in view, she suggested a short drive into the country, followed by a walk through town. "I promised Mama I would pick up some muslin for her this morning," she invented, to give such a dull trip some reason.

She feared her mother was about to reveal her lie, but she did her an injustice. Mrs. Hermitage had read Sally's scheme and was busy to add to it. "And the fish for dinner, Sal," she threw in. The longer Sally could detach Monstuart, the better. "And a leg of mutton from the butcher."

"Mama, the servants can do that!" Sally objected. They were never accustomed to carrying their own groceries home. To sink so low before Lord Monstuart was surely not a good plan.

"As you are going to the shops, dear, it will leave the servants free to polish the silver. The silver wants polishing," Mama insisted. Every candlestick and teapot in the house gleamed like new, but Sally had no intention of playing the undutiful daughter in front of her waiting escort, so she accepted it and even took some satisfaction from the thought of Monstuart's carriage being cluttered with a smelly parcel of fish and a leg of mutton.

Mrs. Hermitage went on to give instructions as to the quantity of turbot required and the degree of marbling necessary to turn the mutton tender. The quantities mentioned told Sally that there was to be more than the family for dinner, but as she had no wish for Monstuart to be one of the projected party, she said not a word about it.

Monstuart's waiting carriage was a handsome black one with a lozenge on the door. Other than the noble emblem, the carriage was no more handsome than the Hermitage's own and elicited no compliments. The trip three miles into the spring countryside passed without any strong unpleasantness. Miss Hermitage occasionally pointed out a particularly fine stand of cedars or patch of wild flowers, but the younger company was not much interested in anything beyond the velvet-lined carriage, and Monstuart's concern with nature seemed hardly greater.

"Very nice," or "charming," he might say, with always that bored look that proclaimed his mood more loudly than words. At length Sally had had enough of trying to introduce some conversation into the trip and said bluntly, "It is clear you take no pleasure in rural beauties, milord. I wonder you are not in London, with the Season just beginning."

"You forget I have been at Beauwood, ma'am. There are some rural beauties there well worth a look. I received my nephew's message while there and am, in fact, on my way to London."

Sally had a pretty good idea what rural beauty at Beauwood was considered worth a look by this urban creature. "Does Lady Dennison go to London as well?" she asked.

"I trust it is her intention."

There was no egging him on to either revelation, dismay, or argument, so like the rest of the group, Sally lapsed into silence till they returned to Ashford. The carriage was sent on, to return in an hour.

Derwent took Melanie's arm and hastened to get beyond earshot of his guardian. Monstuart turned to his companion and asked, with a black brow raised at a querying angle, "Was it worth the trip, to let them have this chance to be alone?"

"Yes, it was worth even that. Whether it is worth having to carry a fish ..." She stopped short, for this was a confession she had not intended making.

"There is the fishmonger's," he pointed out, and, taking her arm, he led her across the street.

"It would be wiser to pick up the fish last," she suggested.

"You're not thinking, Miss Hermitage. If we get it first, I shall have the distinction of carrying it about town. Perhaps *that* will bring you out of your sulks."

"I am not in the sulks."

He regarded her critically. "You're right. That particular expression is called a moue, *n'est-ce pas?* A pout is very becoming to some young ladies." Whether it became this particular one was not stated, as Sally was already heading down the street.

Her nostrils pinched involuntarily when they entered the fish shop. She was unsure whether she would be able to partake of the turbot after seeing it in its unprepared state, with glazed eyes and mottled fins. There was no denying, however, that it gave her great satisfaction to place the parcel in Lord Monstuart's fastidious hands, and still greater pleasure to soon bestow on him as well a large leg of mutton. The pleasure would have been increased had he deigned to show the least of the disgust she was sure he felt, but even when the fish wrapper became noticeably soggy, he did no more than hold it a little away from his superfine jacket and give her a quelling glance that prohibited comment.

The Hermitages had many friends in Ashford. Several were well enough known that they stopped for a chat and an introduction to Lord Monstuart. It was some small pleasure that his lordship was unable to shake hands or remove his hat, for both hands were full of ignominious raw fish and meat.

"I should have had the wits to stick Derwent with this stuff" was the closest he came to complaint. "It would give him a foretaste of this marriage he is bent on contracting."

"It will be enough to put you off from it," Sally replied.

"I need no putting off."

"A misogynist?"

"Not in the least. Say rather misogamist. I have nothing against women but that they make abominable wives."

"It's odd you should say so. I have often wished I had a wife myself, for I think it would be very comfortable to have someone to take care of one's house and bear one's children and be always there to blame when anything goes wrong."

"Your idea has the merit of novelty, at least. I shouldn't mind having a husband to pay the bills and chew out the servants—and carry the fish."

"I shan't trouble you to carry the muslin, at least. I'll undertake that myself. I wouldn't want it to come home smelly."

"You will make an admirable husband, ma'am. I envy your wife."

As this foolishness was going forth, a tall, smiling gentleman in his forties approached. He removed his curled beaver to reveal a long forehead whose length was caused by the recession of his hair to the rear of his scalp. "Miss Hermitage," he said, beaming, and pulled up to talk.

"Why, Mr. Heppleworth, what are you doing with yourself these days? I swear you have deserted us abominably," Sally said. This was the gentleman she had some hopes might make a parti for her mama. He owned a large dairy farm and estate at the edge of town.

"What but ill health could make me desert the Hermitage?" he asked with a look of avid curiosity in Monstuart's direction. Sally performed the introduction but made no motion of walking on at its termination.

"You do not look in the least unhealthy. In the pink of condition, I would say." She smiled.

"It's the hot water that cured me," Heppleworth confided. "Gout, you know. There is nothing like cutting the toenails in hot water to soothe it. Dr. Aylesworth prescribed wearing flannelette booti-kins and staying indoors, but with the hot water and a dozen drops of laudanum to kill the pain, I have put off my bootikins. It was a severe attack. The gout flew from the head to the stomach and gave me a wretched two days, but it is better now. You may look for me at the Hermitage this after-noon." He turned to Monstuart in a conspiratorial way and added, "It is my little conceit to call the ladies' residence the Hermitage. A pun on their name, you see."

"Original." Monstuart smiled. There was no trace of his former boredom but a wicked gleam of appre-ciation.

Heppleworth soon reverted to his ills and cures. "Aylesworth sent me over a quart of excellent paregoric draft. I have siphoned off a cup for your mama. She is subject to a sick stomach, poor old soul."

As her friend was amusing Monstuart, Sally decided not to prolong the visit. "We look forward to seeing you, Mr. Heppleworth."

"Yes, yes, I shall be there for a certainty. You will be home, Miss Hermitage?" he asked with a little jealous dart of the eye to her escort.

"I believe so, but in any case Mama will be there."

"I can come this evening, instead, if you will not be home."

An evening call from Mr. Heppleworth was a thing to be avoided at any cost. About the only danger to health he indulged in was overstaying his visits to the Hermitage. He made up for it by sleeping in till noon, but the fact was his evening visit lasted well into the night and often till early morning. His peculiar insistence that she be on hand to receive him sent a question shivering through Sally. Could Mama be right that it was she, Sally, that the old fool had in his eye?

"Oh, no! Do come this afternoon. I shall be there," she said, and immediately took her leave.

"You should have reminded him to bring his bootikins," Monstuart said as they walked on to the drapery shop. His arms were becoming tired from holding the parcels at an awkward angle, and his temper was not wearing well.

"It wasn't necessary. He keeps a spare pair at our house."

"What an old quiz."

"He is one of our best friends," she announced, and gave him such a glare that he said not another word of denigration.

"We have half an hour till we meet your sister and Derwent. Is there somewhere we might sit down and get this load off my hands?" Monstuart asked.

"I told you to buy the fish last," she scolded.

"True, but you didn't tell me you intended saddling me with half a sheep as well. There is a tea shop ahead. Let us go in and sit down."

They entered the homey little tearoom. A delicious aroma of yeast, cinnamon, and sugar hung on the air, and at several small tables the buzz of gossip increased. Derwent and Melanie were already ensconced at a table near the rear. Sally looked at her escort with suspicion.

"This is fortuitous," he assured her.

Sally didn't believe a word of it, especially when he walked quickly to their table and placed his burden on any empty chair before offering her a seat. Half the single hour allotted to the lovers was completely wasted. Not an amorous word was exchanged between them from that moment on, and very few words of any other sort.

The burden of talk fell on the elder couple. With Monstuart in a bad mood from carrying the foods and Sally in the boughs at his sly trick, the half hour lasted long. Derwent couldn't even offer Melanie his arm upon leaving, for both parcels had been summarily placed in his hands. In order to deliver the groceries, Derwent, with Melanie, entered the house where it was his custom to take a

52

good many of his meals. It was the greatest wish of every one of the young people that Monstuart go on home alone, but he got down from the carriage and entered the house with them, obviously bent on watching Derwent every moment that it should be possible. They were both invited to lunch, but with a scathing look at his uncle, Derwent declined.

"You will be having company this afternoon. We'll leave," Monstuart said. Before leaving, he approached Mrs. Hermitage and had a short private conversation with her.

As soon as the gentlemen were out the door, both daughters inquired what he had said. "He is reconsidering!" The happy mother beamed and laughed aloud in delight.

"There is nothing to consider," Sally said. "Derwent has firmly offered. It's all settled."

"Derwent speaks of waiting a year or so," Melanie confessed. "He dislikes to live on our money, you know. His uncle told him it was not at all the thing."

"Much he cares about that!" Sally fired up. "It's a trick to stave him off till he changes his mind."

"Oh, dear, and the romance is bound to come off the boil with Monstuart forever hanging around," Mrs. Hermitage said.

"He won't change his mind," Melanie exclaimed.

"Derwent wouldn't have to live on our money if Monstuart would give him some of his own," Sally said. "It's outrageous that a full-grown man like Derwent must grovel to that monster."

"He is reconsidering, dear," her mother repeated, placing great faith that the reconsideration would have good results. "If he permits the marriage to go forth, he will give Derwent some of his money, and that would be so much better than having to spend our own."

Miss Hermitage was far from convinced. "It's an excuse to stick around and scotch the romance if he can. His blighting presence is enough to cool down Romeo and Juliet." And Derwent, she knew, fell in and out of love easily. "When does Derwent return?" she asked Melanie.

"Not this afternoon. His uncle has seen to that." Mellie pouted. "What company did he mean would be coming?"

Sally explained that Mr. Heppleworth was to call, a message that was received without a single shout of glee. "At least he's coming in the afternoon" was her mother's unenthusiastic response.

"A pity you couldn't warm up to him, Mama," Sally said.

"It's not me he comes to see."

"I hope you are not implying I am the one he has in his eye, Mama!" Sally objected, but she was coming to terms with that fact that it was so. Her friendliness, instigated to show Heppleworth he would be entirely welcome as a father, had led him astray.

"Perhaps Derwent will come this evening," Mrs. Hermitage said, to remove the pout from Mellie's face. "He would not at all enjoy being here when Heppleworth is telling us about his gout this afternoon, love."

"Yes, but where *will* he be?" Melanie countered. "His uncle will take him to visit some other girl. I know it."

"That's what he's up to!" Sally exclaimed, and

wondered that she hadn't thought of it herself. She didn't continue, as she noticed that her agreement had thrown Melanie deeper into the sulks, but her mind was actively running over the likely young ladies in whose direction Monstuart might try to divert Derwent's interest.

The afternoon was as dreary as Mr. Heppleworth could make it with his litany of ailments. His tired eyes rested often on Sally, in a way that spoke silently of his intentions. Dinner was little better, with Melanie wilting about like a tired bloom. The evening yawned before them. When the knocker sounded, Miss Hermitage hoped it was Derwent, even if his guardian was with him. In fact, she felt an explicable little hope that Monstuart had come as well.

Chapter Five

Sally was not aware of it, but her lively face wore an expression of anticipation that changed to a tentative smile when she saw Monstuart's dark head looming behind Derwent at the doorway to the Rose Saloon. Nor was she consciously aware that the uncle looked first toward her, but she felt some little satisfaction when he took up a seat beside her. His first talk was directed to her mama, some trifling inquiry as to whether she had enjoyed her fish, which gave Sally time enough to wonder that she was not in a worse mood to see Monstuart again in their house.

But she was not in a bad mood. In fact, she was wishing he would stop talking to Mama and pay some attention to her. This was a great enough change from her former feeling that some rationalization must be found for it. She regarded his sleek black head, the back of which was her view at the moment, and his wide shoulders, covered in a jacket that was certainly the work of Weston. No wonder if she should be diverted to have a city gentleman to talk to after enduring two hours of Mr. Hippleworth's gout, she decided.

The black head soon turned in her direction, and its owner caught her studying him with a pensive expression. "What's the matter?" he asked. "Have I got my hair mussed?"

"No, I shouldn't think you ever go into public without a careful perusal of your toilette from all angles," she retorted, piqued to have been caught out in her examination.

"Very true. I have been pirouetting in front of my mirror this past half hour and can't think what detail escaped me."

"No detail. I have been admiring your barbering."

"May I return the compliment and say I admire your coiffure? *La Grecque* suits you very well." Monstuart took care that no hint of admiration lit his eyes or lightened his bored tone. "You are wise to continue wearing it, even though it is no longer considered the highest kick of fashion in London," he added.

Miss Hermitage was not deceived into taking this for a compliment. Like any provincial lady, she was sensitive to the charge of being behind the style. His sly set-down was as good as an invitation to battle. "I must apologize if my antiquated hair style has offended you."

"I have most particularly told you I admire it," he pointed out.

"You have also told me it is out of style!"

"No, only out of fashion. Not all fashions are good. The macédoine of lace and ribbons and spangles often seen nowadays in evening toilettes, for example, is quite hideous." He glanced at Sally's severe gown.

She immediately inferred another insult. "Much I care about London," she scoffed.

The dark eyes lingering on her mobile face held an unconscious tinge of admiration. "Were we there this evening, we would have something more lively to look forward to than a game of what, for want of a better word, we shall call chess. Kean is playing at Drury Lane. I have not been in town for some time, but I seem to recall there were some interesting balls offered this week. The Meltons, I think, the Melbournes certainly, and Lady Besswood's ball, which she calls a rout. There is a new opera being premiered, and a ridotto at—"

"The week has only seven days, milord. Even such a confirmed hedonist as you could hardly take in more than you've already mentioned," she said curtly. Her longing for these treats made her peevish.

"You underestimate me. For propriety's sake, I've omitted some of my less worthy social doings."

"For what reason do you hint at them, if propriety is of any interest to you at all?"

His dark eyes studied her till she felt uncomfortable. "You're not seven years old. I suspect you have an inkling how the world wags."

Sally lifted an imperious brow and stared him down. Why was he speaking in this broad way to her, as though she were married, or a lady of advanced years? "Do you want to play cards or not?" she asked.

"No, but I want even less to sit and watch my nephew make a jackanapes of himself. What do they

say, do you suppose, for hours in that little corner?"
They both turned their attention to the inglenook.

"I'm surprised you have to ask. You have just
implied that, despite your misogamy, you are no
stranger to dalliance."

A rakish smile took possession of his face. "If
that's the way he's carrying on, I'll go right over
and box his ears," he said. That smile lent a new
aura to Monstuart's dark, rather forbidding aspect.
It hinted at intrigue and caused a warm flush to
invade her being. "My sort of dalliance wouldn't
suit your *sister* at all," he added, staring at her.

Sally colored at the implication that it would suit
her. She decided to misunderstand him. "Derwent's
sort seems to suit her very well."

His smile dwindled to an ironic grin. "All to do
with pledges of eternal devotion, broken hearts if I
manage to lure him off for a spell, and that sort of
carry-on, I wager."

"I see nothing wrong in that."

His frown managed to include both disbelief and
disapproval. "It is ridiculous for a puppy to be
promising eternal love at the height of an infatuation that won't outlive the season. Of course, love
is madness, and madmen aren't held accountable
for their promises."

"This one will be," she cautioned.

When Sally looked toward the grate, she found
Derwent's expression not far removed from lunacy.
The two were sitting close together, smiling and
occasionally saying a word, as they have been for a
month. How could her sister endure it night after
night?

When Mrs. Hermitage arose to get her netting

box, Monstuart said, "Would you have a spare needle? I'm about ready to try my hand at that embroidery business."

"Why do you remain in Ashford, if you find it so boring?" Sally asked.

"I think you have an idea why I stick." His eyes moved slowly from the grate to study Sally. His smile was enigmatic but less satirical than before.

"You're wasting your time. You can't stop this marriage. You will look foolish in the extreme if he must borrow from us to finance his first years of marriage."

"I shall look nohow—in that extremely unlikely case. Shall we play with the chess pieces, or would you rather tackle something else this evening?"

"I'm a bit of a dab at backgammon," she suggested.

"I don't know the game."

"Piquet?"

He nodded. "A shilling a point?"

"You forget I am a pauper. A penny a point."

"Chicken stakes."

Sally leveled a cool stare at him. "What stakes would you expect in a chicken roost?"

"That ill-chosen speech has been relayed by your mother, I see. I have apologized to her, and now I apologize to you," he said, but curtly, with no air of contrition. "A penny a point it is."

"You of all people ought not to encourage me to outrun the grocer, as I plan to dump all my expenses in Derwent's lap."

"I see we both assume *I* shall be the winner," he said blandly.

They rose and walked to the games table, where Sally drew out cards and handed them to her partner to be dealt. During a game that lasted for over an hour, she was soundly trounced. She liked to win, but in spite of this, she had not found an evening to pass so quickly and pleasantly for some time. Monstuart could be maddening, but he could also be a highly entertaining partner. The battle between them added a welcome spice to it all and gave her a worthy conversational opponent. It came as a shock and a disappointment when her partner began to yawn into his fist and suggested he had had enough of cards.

"Even with the inducement of my colossal winnings," he added, sweeping a few coins of small denomination into his hand and pocketing them. "Did the pharmacopoeia in breeches we met today come to call?" he asked.

"Mr. Heppleworth was here this afternoon," she replied.

"Was Miss Hermitage home to greet him, as he so ardently hopped?"

"Yes, I was."

"Is he an example of the suitors available to you at Ashford?"

She felt an unwelcome blush stain her cheeks, that Monstuart should see the paltry quality of her suitors. "I have always preferred older gentlemen."

"Older is a relative term. Older than what? Watch your answer closely, Miss Hermitage. It cannot have escaped your sharp eyes that I am older than you."

Her eyes snapped angrily. Was he daring to imply she had set her cap at him? Had she betrayed the growing interest?

"Caught without an answer, Miss Hermitage? Use that much-vaunted intelligence. You prefer white hair, perhaps? A touch of the gout?"

"I prefer white hair to town bronze, in any case."

He rose and hunched his elegant shoulders non-chalantly. "We have already discussed the impossibility of accounting for taste on a former occasion. Now I bid you good evening." On this speech he went to join the others.

Derwent was just rising to take his leave. "Tomorrow at six, then." He smiled to Mrs. Hermitage.

"I hope you will join us for dinner tomorrow evening as well, Lord Monstuart," the mother said. "We are having a few guests in—Mr. Heppleworth and the Crosbys."

"I have been hoping for an opportunity to know Mr. Heppleworth better. I will be delighted to come," Monstuart said without a trace of a smile or a blush. Sally stared at him, but he kept his head averted, talking to her mother for another moment.

He only turned back to her when he took his leave. His satirical grin might have been caused by the invitation, or the fact that he was ushering Derwent out the door at such an early hour. It certainly did not match his polite murmurs of having had a delightful evening.

"I don't see why you had to include Monstuart," Melanie scolded as soon as the ladies were alone.

"He is reconsidering, my dear," her mother reminded her. "It would not do to be rude at such a time. He hinted, just before he left, that if he finds you girls to behave with propriety, he will allow the match."

"There's nothing improper in what we do!" Melanie exclaimed.

It would have been difficult to level such a charge against Melanie. Sally often wished for more social awareness from her sister. She thought perhaps Monstuart wanted a more polished bride for his nephew. As a peer, he would be meeting persons from a high social level, and a wife that did no more than smile at her husband would be small asset. But her mother's remark caused her to wonder whether it was Melanie's manners he referred to.

"He has the greatest dislike of pertness," Mrs. Hermitage mentioned. To accuse Melanie of pertness was like accusing a sloth of speed. When the mother slid a questioning look at her elder daughter and said, "I hope you were not pert, Sal," Monstuart's meaning became perfectly clear.

Indignation burned deep, and Sally flared up. "Is that what he was whispering in your ear, Mama?"

"He didn't say so, not in the least, but as he spent all his time with you, I did just wonder whether it was not you he meant. You do have a habit of saying things you ought not to, no denying."

"He's a fine one to talk."

"Oh, Sal, you *have* been flirting with him," her mother charged.

"Flirting with that jackdaw? I'd as soon flirt with a—a weasel!" she declared, and flounced from the room. But when she was alone, she had to ask herself in good earnest whether she was not guilty. Her tongue had the habit of running free, but so far from trying to dampen it, Monstuart had egged her on at every turn. He was *trying* to make her behave ill, to have an excuse to find fault with the family! Knowing Melanie and Mama were unexceptionable, he had found out the weak link and concentrated his efforts on her. And how easily she had fallen into the trap. Like a Bartholomew Baby, she had been cozened into behaving with an unbecoming freedom.

His repeatedly suggesting that she would like London—that, too, was a trick. He wanted to be able to tell Derwent she intended attaching herself to him and Melanie. He had been wise enough to see there was no love lost between Derwent and her. She could almost hear what he would say to his nephew: "A solicitor's undowered daughter is disadvantage enough. But a pert sister who battens herself on you and leads your bride astray . . ." That's how he would twist things.

Her blood fairly boiled when she thought of it, and she longed to retaliate. A dozen brazen speeches occurred to her. If Derwent was not led astray by a philandering uncle, it was not likely his wife would be led astray by her sister. If Melanie was so biddable as that, why had she remained unspoiled for so long? And furthermore, Sally had no intention of living with them! An occasional visit, a few weeks during the Season, was all she ever had in mind.

After hearing Monstuart boast of his social whirl, Sally wanted those few weeks very much. And she wanted it from such an unexceptionable base as her sister, married to Lord Derwent, would provide. What was the point of hiring a set of rooms in some apartment house in Upper Grosvenor Square? She wanted Melanie's marriage for her sister's sake, and there was no reason a small benefit should not trickle down to Sally. Melanie *would* marry Derwent, and she *would* visit them. Strong as the temptation was to come to cuffs with Monstuart, she would behave with the greatest propriety he had ever seen. She would utter not a word that might not be said before the twelve apostles and their mothers.

The next meeting with him would be her mother's dinner party. She would make Mr. Heppleworth her dinner partner and her conversation partner after dinner. It would take a miracle to make Mr. Heppleworth misbehave, but she must not encourage the old fool to think she loved him. Let Lord Monstuart raise his black brows and quiz her as much as he liked; she would not be betrayed into impropriety.

Chapter Six

No definite meeting between Derwent and Melanie was set for any time before the dinner party,
but there was a general expectation that he would
not allow nearly twenty-four hours to roll by without a glimpse of his beloved, nor did he. He was
there the next morning at ten forty-five, striking a
balance between his own preferred time and that
of his uncle, who was again with him. Monstuart's
city barbering and tailoring received no smiling
welcome this morning. Sally sat silent in a corner,
determined to be civil. He asked her to drive out
again, and she bit back the rejoinder that she was
surprised he should suggest it, when yesterday's
drive gave him so little pleasure.

"I'm afraid I'm busy this morning," she replied.
From having been in the saloon since ten-thirty.
waiting for him, she knew the gentlemen had come
in two carriages, and her going was not necessary.
She did wonder why he wanted to be alone with her
and could only conclude he intended to step up his
plan of luring her into indiscretion.

"Setting up a new tambour frame?" he asked politely.

"It is my sister and Mama who are the needle-women," she reminded him.

"And you, if memory serves, like reading. What book have you discovered that you can't be drawn away? Byron—it must be Byron. You have not fallen behind in your literary fashion, at any rate. All the young ladies are hiding the new cantos of *Childe Harold* from their mamas."

"I am reading a very exciting drama by Hannah More," she said, lying through her teeth and enjoying it.

Monstuart looked for a telltale movement of her lips and saw only a prim line. "Exciting in the same sentence as Hannah More? That sounds like a contradiction in terms to me."

"I enjoy her uplifting theological exercises."

Monstuart didn't answer immediately but just lifted his quizzing glass and stared at her till she became nervous. "I had hoped you might be kind enough to accompany me to Canterbury," he said next.

The weather was particularly fine. A drive of fifteen or so miles to Canterbury in Monstuart's elegant carriage and luncheon at a restaurant were a strong inducement. But as the outing offered so much opportunity for pertness, Sally declined.

He never for a moment thought he was really being refused. She was playing hard to get, a game he knew well and rather enjoyed. "We could visit the cathedral—Hannah More would approve of that," he tempted with a smile that had nothing to do with cathedrals.

Sally thought Hannah herself would find that smile hard to resist, but she was made of sterner stuff. "Living so close, we have toured the cathedral several times. I do recommend it to you, however, if you haven't been there. It is considered a particularly fine example of perpendicular architecture, I believe."

"I've paid my duty visit to admire it. That removes the onus of having to do so today. My real reason for the trip is to visit an everything store and find some games to help us wile away the evenings," he tempted, but still she demurred.

Finally convinced that Sally was adamant, he rose with a questioning look. "It seems we must rely on a recital of Mr. Heppleworth's assorted ills for our evening's entertainment, unless you can suggest something I pick up while there?"

Sally had not a single suggestion to make.

"You won't be needing any fish—mutton?" he teased, trying to beguile her into a smile before leaving. He discerned a glitter in her green eyes and waited expectantly for her retort.

"No, thank you," she said calmly.

No jibes, no sparks, no taunts. "I didn't expect my advice to your mother would have this effect!" He scowled and finally left, alone.

Sally was well satisfied with her fortitude. He had thought her temper so unstable that she would be betrayed into even worse behavior than usual, and had the barefaced audacity to say as much. That evening she would be even more polite, let him goad as he might. She was in good spirits for half an hour, till she began envisioning the trip she had missed, at which point she turned waspish.

As afternoon advanced into evening, her spirits rose once more. Determined to be acceptable, she wore her least dashing gown and wished it were even less dashing. It was an elegant robe of deep mulberry that brought her ivory neck and shoulders into prominence without suggesting any impropriety. Around her throat she wore the small strand of diamonds Papa had given her on her seventeenth birthday, and had her hair dressed à la Grecque. To change it would suggest she cared for Monstuart's opinion.

Looking at her image in the mirror, Sally gurgled softly to herself to consider that this fashionable lady was about to play the role of Bath Miss. She hunched her impertinent shoulders and danced downstairs when she heard the knocker through her open door. The gentlemen being shown in by Rinkin caught only a glimpse of her laughing eyes. The minute she recognized Monstuart's dark head and wide shoulders, she pokered up and advanced at a stately gait to make them welcome. Her curtsy was the stiffest curtsy ever performed by her lithe young body.

The single glimpse he had seen of Sally's habitual self had already put a smile on Monstuart's saturnine face. He bowed, flickering a practiced eye over her toilette. "Enchanting," he murmured.

"Mulberry is still being worn in the provinces," she replied, and led the guests into the Rose Saloon with a word tossed over her shoulder to Derwent to assure him Melanie would be down presently. Little tendrils of black curls fell below the Greek knot and nestled on her white neck, causing sufficient interest to Monstuart that he was still smiling when she showed him a seat.

"Did you have a pleasant drive to Canterbury?" she inquired.

"Not so pleasant as it would have been if you had accompanied me, but tolerable. I found a book I hope you will accept," he said, and handed her a small volume bound in Russian leather.

Surprised, she glanced at the title and saw it to be a play by Hannah More entitled *The Fatal Falsehood*. "A dramatic tragedy by your favorite author," he said, his dark eyes laughing.

Sally refused to recognize any significance in the title and thanked him calmly. "I look forward to reading it. This is one that hasn't come my way before. I have just been dipping into her *Thoughts on the Manners of the Great* and found it most amusing," she said, not betraying by an accent that she was retaliating for his *daring* to hint she had lied to say she was busy.

"That's *Thoughts on the Importance of the Manners of the Great*, ma'am, if I'm not mistaken," Monstuart pointed out. "Not quite so apropos—from your point of view—but a very good riposte. I congratulate you."

Her raised brows and blank look were meant to imply she was lost at his rejoinder, but as some widening of her great green eyes accompanied the gesture, Monstuart failed to perceive anything but their beauty and smiled on, bemused. "Is the wandering pharmacopoeia not here yet?'" he asked. "I made sure he was the sort who would be awkwardly on time and rushed Derwent out of the house with his cravat untied in a race to beat him."

It provided an excuse to include Derwent in the conversation. "I see you have managed to get it tied, and must congratulate you on doing it so well in a jostling carriage," she said.

"Your congratulations are misdirected, Miss Hermitage," Monstuart informed her. "It was I who executed the Oriental you are admiring. I wear the same style myself. Perhaps you would care to admire mine as well?"

This venture earned him a brief glance and a very mild "Lovely.

"Where did you and Melanie go this afternoon?" she asked Derwent. Melanie had already related every stop and every flower seen, but Sally was determined to converse with the less interesting gentleman, and trying to talk to Derwent was always a trial.

"We drove toward Dover," he said. "It was very nice, with all the spring flowers and sunshine and whatnot. I picked Mellie a bouquet."

"Every flower of which will be pressed before her head hits the pillow this evening," Monstuart prophesied with an air of ennui.

Sally knew they were already being flattened between the pages of stout volumes, for she had been asked to help find books for the job. "What a novel idea. I shall suggest it to my sister," she replied with a determined smile.

"It was only daisies and buttercups," Derwent said idly.

"And bluebells," Sally added, then looked quickly away as she received a knowing shot from the other gentleman.

"I wonder what ladies do with all the bushels of

flowers they press annually," Monstuart asked of no one in particular. "A distressing number of them find their way behind frames. Do you press flowers and make arrangements, Miss Hermitage?"

"No, I am not at all artistic."

"Neither are most of the ladies who stick a bunch of dry and discolored weeds into a frame. For some reason the fact that they did it themselves is considered sufficient justification for hanging the results on the wall to offend the aesthetic sensitivities of their guests. I think there ought to be a law against it. The anti-dried flower framing law, it would be called. Why don't you suggest it in your maiden speech in the House, Derwent? You will earn the undying gratitude of every man in the kingdom."

"He is only funning," Derwent told Sally. "Monty is a Whig. He has an odd sense of humor."

Sally cast an understanding smile at the lover, who hardly knew what to say. They both found themselves staring at the bunch of dried May flowers arranged by his unartistic beloved not a month ago and now decorating the wall. Aware of a stretching silence, Sally said, "You are not sentimental, Monstuart."

"Thank you, ma'am," he inserted quickly.

She ignored him and continued talking to Derwent, who was astonished to receive so much friendly condescension from Sally. "To persons of sensibility, the fact that the work was done by a loved one, in memory of a shared experience, constitutes the point of it."

"Absolutely."

Monstuart, determined to spoil her disquisition,

said, "I'm glad to hear there's *some* point. One trembles to think of the results if they took into their heads to frame every shared book and box of bonbons and tearstained handkerchief that speaks of their love."

"They could hardly frame a consumed box of candy, in any case," Sally snapped. Her color rose and her eyes sparkled in vexation.

"They don't usually consume the box," he pointed out. "Unless they happen to be goats, of course."

The supporters of sentiment exchanged a commiserating smile. "I make sure Melanie will make a lovely arrangement from the daisies and buttercups," Sally said.

"And bluebells," Monstuart added. "You should break down and buy the lady a bouquet of roses if she is a lover of flowers, Derwent."

"Buying is not at all the same thing," Sally pointed out. "It is the gathering of the blooms together that makes up the memory. A quiet stroll through sun-dappled fields . . ."

Derwent was amazed to hear such good sense from her. "You have hit it dead on, Miss Hermitage."

"It has been my experience that ladies are very well satisfied with a dozen or two of roses from a mildew-dappled florist." Monstuart insisted.

"There are ladies and there are ladies," Sally said ever so gently. Her speaking eyes held a touch of innuendo.

"Very true." Monstuart nodded. "Some of them are even sensible enough to prefer a less perishable gift than a flower. And what is so imperishable as a diamond?"

"But we are discussing *ladies*, milord," Sally reminded him, still gentle.

"I was beginning to think it was geese or some other bird-witted creatures we were talking about."

As the phrase "bird-witted creatures" was uttered, Miss Melanie and her mama entered the saloon on cue and welcomed their guests.

"Is Heppleworth not here yet?" Mrs. Hermitage asked. "I made sure when I saw the hats and canes in the hall he was here. He always will land in on the dot, like a farmer."

Monstuart gave her a quizzing smile. "My apologies for being on time, ma'am." It was laughed away with the assurance that Mrs. Hermitage was sorry she was late. "Next time I shall follow London punctuality. I see you and your daughters have not quite broken city habits yet."

Alert to a trap, Sally declared that she adored the country and wouldn't leave it for anything.

"Why, Sal, what a plumper!" her mother exclaimed. "I'm sure if you've bemoaned missing the Season once, you've done it seven times a week."

"Even on Sunday, eh?" Monstuart asked archly.

Having no reply to save her face, Miss Hermitage was obliged not to hear the question, nor to realize Monstuart went on looking at her, waiting for an answer. "I wonder what can be keeping Mr. Heppleworth," she said.

"Very likely the gout, or it could be an upset stomach, or a stop at the chemist shop," her mother suggested. Monstuart watched Sally closely, ready to smile if she glanced his way, but she was busy pressing an imaginary wrinkle from her skirt with her fingers.

When Heppleworth arrived a few moments later, it proved to be no medical errand but a social one that had delayed him. He had stopped at the sweet shop to purchase two large, gaudy boxes of bon-bons, one for Mrs. Hermitage and one for Sally. "Sweets for the sweet," he said, presenting them with a flourish and wishing at the moment of truth that he had either gone whole hog and got one for Melanie, too, or had the courage to limit his gifts to Sally. The arrival of Monstuart on the scene had caused him to step up his desultory courting.

"How nice!" Mrs. Hermitage said. "My, two whole pounds—this is a surprise. You shouldn't have, Mr. Heppleworth."

"Thank you," Sally said quietly. She wished the box were not quite so large, the satin covering not quite so red, the quantity of lace paper and bows not so great. It was the sort of gift shopkeepers presented to their lovers and it did not escape her eyes that Monstuart was biting his lips in amusement. She felt less inclined to favor Mr. Heppleworth with her company after this gift. When Monstuart got a step ahead of him to the sofa beside her, she was half-glad.

"It will look spectacular in a frame," he told her in a quiet aside, glancing at the box. "I suggest a very plain one, to counter the extravagance of the lid. Really, your lack of artistry will never be noticed."

It required a deal of self-command to take this in humor, but Sally managed it. "A lovely thought, is it not?" she asked.

"What, sweets for the sweet? Lovely, perhaps,

highly original, of course, but inappropriate for Miss Hermitage."

"I think you are not being nice, milord," she said through thin lips.

"It is costing you more than it's worth to go on being nice in the face of such wanton provocation as this," he told her, again eyeing the vulgar box. "You'll need a dose of that paregoric draft. May I ask what accounts for this unaccustomed fit of propriety?"

"I hope I am not accustomed to behaving with anything but propriety!"

A brief, puzzled frown flitted over Monstuart's swarthy face. Then he turned his attention to Heppleworth. Was it even remotely conceivable that Sally was putting on this show of niceness for the old slice's benefit? Surely he was mistaken.

The Crosbys soon arrived, and dinner was called. Mrs. Hermitage set an elegant table, with two courses and two removes. With the increase to the party of the Crosbys, a conversable couple of good breeding and broad interests, the meal was a success. After dinner, Mrs. Crosby kept Melanie entertained by asking her questions about Derwent till the gentlemen joined them.

At this point, someone suggested a round of whist, and while the table was being set up there was some discussion as to who would partner Mrs. Hermitage against the Crosbys. Derwent was, of course, excused, which left Monstuart and Heppleworth. It was patently obvious that both wished to cry off and have Miss Hermitage to himself. She had only to engage one in conversation and the other would fall victim to the table. She was loath to be stuck with Heppleworth for an hour or two, yet wouldn't satisfy Monstuart to choose him. Heppleworth, with more nerve and less manners, carried the day.

"I can't settle down to cards so soon after a heavy meal," he decreed. "My stomach is always upset till I have my gargle of tea. I must sit quietly and digest my food."

With a bland countenance and a burning temper, Monstuart begged permission to be allowed to be the fourth player. Heppleworth aided the heavy meal's digestion by topping it off with a quarter of a pound of gooey bonbons. Miss Hermitage realized she should be relieved that she was spared Monstuart's company. She had been on tiptoes to light into him all evening, and now she was safe. He would be at cards for an hour at least, probably more.

During the whole time, he never once glanced at her. He looked occasionally toward his nephew and Melanie, but Sally felt she might as well not have been there for all the attention he paid to her.

It seemed hours before the tea tray was brought in. If she could have drawn her sister and Derwent into the conversation, it would have relieved the tedium, but repeated hints and two direct requests brought no results. She was stuck to entertain Mr. Heppleworth by herself and eat at least a few of his bonbons, for her kept shoving the box at her.

Worst of all, it was becoming perfectly clear that she was the object of his affection. Subtle hints were dropped as to the pleasure of being "alone with her at last, suitably chaperoned, of course." "In the not too far distant future, I hope we may, with all propriety, dispense with a chaperon entirely." At length, Sally could endure it no longer.

She did the unthinkable. She barged in on the duo by the fireside and made them talk to her, or at least listen. Heppleworth hobbled over, too, but he was quiet. She felt as welcome as rain at a picnic, but she stayed with them till the tea was brought in. Sally usurped her mother's prerogative and hastened to the table to pour. There was only one chair at the table, so Heppleworth could not join her.

Mrs. Crosby, a lady of some sophistication, had seen enough of Sally's problem that she took a seat beside Mr. Heppleworth and charmed him into a discussion of all his recent ills. When all the cups were filled, Sally took hers to the farthest side of the room from her aged pursuer.

Monstuart immediately rose and joined her. "My turn," he said with a teasing smile. "To hound and harass you," he explained when she gave him a dazed look. "But I promise not to force a single bonbon down your throat. They're ghastly. The square ones have chunks of bitter orange peel in them."

"I know. I had four," she said, and was too weary to wonder whether she was being indiscreet.

"One would have been sufficient to show your good will in the matter. You don't want to *encourage* him." He waited expectantly for some denial of this ridiculous charge.

Sally sat with her spine stiff and her expression schooled to primness. "Why should I not? He is very eligible. Mr. Heppleworth owns Tintagel Farm, a vast enterprise. He raises milchers."

"That would explain his bovine manner, but it does not explain your complacence to his courting."

Why should she "explain" anything to this interloper? "Did you enjoy your card game?" she asked.

"No."

"I'm sorry to hear it."

"I think not. You're delighted that I, too, have been miserable for the past sixty minutes. Don't let politeness stand in the way of our enjoying at least the dog end of this awful evening."

The temptation to give vent to some of her pent-up vexation was strong, but with a final effort, Sally resisted. "I'm sorry you have had a flat time."

Monstuart's brows drew together in perplexity. "Are you not feeling well, Miss Hermitage?"

"I feel fine."

"You aren't behaving like yourself. I lay the blame in Heppleworth's dish—er, box."

"Why do you disparage him?" she said rather loudly. "And please lower your voice, or Mr. Heppleworth will hear you."

"You are the one who raised her voice. And in any case, would it be a calamity if he caught a glimpse of the *real* you?"

She tossed her head boldly. "Of course not. He is sufficiently smitten to withstand my manner."

A few more efforts at flirtation were roundly snubbed. Monstuart was not accustomed to playing second fiddle to anyone, and to find himself second to an aging invalid with neither conversation nor looks put his back up. He decided to play his trump. "I shall be leaving the neighborhood tomorrow," he said. That should jar her out of her smugness.

79

A look of alarm leaped into her eyes. "Do you take Derwent with you?"

That was her only interest in him, his control over Derwent. "Good idea. I'm glad you thought of it."

"But you said you would reconsider!"

"So I shall—at Beauwood."

Monstuart rose and left, taking Derwent with him. As soon as the other guests left—and it was quite late before Heppleworth was finally ejected—Sally told the family the startling news.

"Derwent is coming to call tomorrow. Monstuart was only trying to frighten you," Melanie said. "Let him return to his mistress's houseparty. I wish he would *stay* there."

"I wish we knew Lady Dennison's feeling about all this," Mrs. Hermitage said worriedly. "She could be some kin to Lady Mary DeBeirs, for all we know. Oh, dear, now what shall we do?"

"Let us go to bed," Sally suggested.

"But what has put Monstuart out of sorts?" the mother persisted. "Did you say anything to him, Sally? I thought you looked strangely morose all evening. You didn't offend him, I hope?"

"I didn't say a word that could possibly offend anyone," Sally exclaimed. "Pray don't lay it in *my* dish. Monstuart was looking for an excuse to forbid the match, and since he couldn't find one, he's going to forbid it anyway. I don't know why he stayed so long, beast of a man."

On this angry speech she flounced upstairs.

Chapter Seven

The most surprised party in the house when Derwent actually appeared for his appointment was Sally. She was sure his uncle would whisk him off to court Lady Mary and her fortune. Strangely enough, this troubled her less than the knowledge that Monstuart had returned to Lady Dennison.

"It seems to me he was a very poor choice of guardian for you, Derwent," she said. "I have often heard Papa say the first prerequisite of a guardian is that he have high morals. I, for one, would not pay a libertine like Monstuart the least heed."

"He told me you'd say that." Derwent nodded. "The fact is he says it is not all entertainment at Beauwood. There is some Whig skullduggery going on as well. In any case, I told him I would not do anything rash till he returned, to be rid of him."

"Does that ugly word 'rash' refer to your marriage with Melanie?" Sally demanded. Melanie shot him an offended look.

"Certainly not!" he answered promptly. "That is—I daresay that is what he meant. Well, it was, but I do not consider it rash. I would be rash *not* to marry her while I have the chance, in my opinion.

"You promised not to do anything rash, Derwent," Sally replied, half in jest. "In that case, you had best marry her, then."

Melanie was never much inclined to appreciate a jest. Her blue eyes widened with interest as she gazed a question at her fiancé. "She's right, Derwent," she said.

"No, really! I was joking!" Sally exclaimed.

"It is better than running away to Gretna Green, at least, and that is what—that is . . ." Melanie came to a breathless stop while Derwent squirmed in his seat.

"Derwent—you spoke of waiting a year!" Mrs. Hermitage gasped. "You cannot be so foolish as to even *consider* Gretna Green. To be married over the anvil—it would sink you. And it is not at all necessary. Monstuart is reconsidering."

"We only spoke of Gretna Green the first evening Monty came and kicked up such a dust," Derwent assured her. He shook his head diffidently. "He was dashed angry again last night. It wouldn't surprise me in the least if he does forbid the match. The money, I mean, for he can't forbid the marriage, exactly. He often pretends he is going to give permission for things, but in the end he manages to put a spoke into it somehow or other. I expect where he is really gone is to Chêne Baie to be in touch with the DeBeirses, to bring Lady Mary here or some such thing."

A shock of dreadful alarm ran through the room. Even Derwent seemed to be affected by it. "I cannot like Gretna Green," Mrs. Hermit said weakly.

Sally was stunned into silence, which she put to use to scan the situation. Before long, she had taken her decision, and in a roomful of indecisive people, she was listened to. "We are a parcel of fools!" she said. "Derwent is not a minor, nor is Melanie. They do not have to dart to Gretna Green. They can be married very respectably right here, in the bride's home."

"Yes, dear," her mother pointed out, "but the banns take two weeks, and before then Monstuart will come pouncing back to prevent it."

"It can be done in a day with special license. Now, you know there is nothing havey-cavey in *that*, Mama. Dozens of people do it for a small wedding."

"But I want a large wedding," Melanie declared.

"If you want any wedding at all to Derwent, you had best be satisified with a small one," her mama warned.

Melanie considered this for a moment. "It would be romantic," Derwent urged. "And once it is done, you know, he could do nothing about it."

"He could withhold your money for two years," Sally reminded him. She was already feeling some qualms as to whether she'd done the right thing to rush the wedding forward.

"We weren't planning to wait two years, I promise you," Derwent said. "I mean two years! As far as that goes, even Monstuart would prefer a quiet, private, decent wedding to a dash to the Border."

Mrs. Hermitage fanned herself vigorously. "I wish you would not say such horrid things, Derwent." Then she turned to the most sensible member of the group and continued. "What is to be done, Sal? We cannot have this pair romping off to Gretna

Green. It would quite ruin your chances, to say nothing of Mellie's reputation. Yet Derwent feels Monstuart will never give his approval. It looks as though we must give them a wedding, and if necessary use our own money till Monstuart relents."

All faces turned eagerly to hear her answer. Sally had only to say "let's do it," and the thing would be done. Yet something held her back, and that something, she knew, was the fear of Monstuart's wrath. There was an element in the situation that angered her—either that she feared Monstuart or that the onus of a final decision had shifted to her shoulders. She replied curtly, "It's not my decision. Ask Derwent—he's of age. It is for him to decide—and, of course, Mellie."

Her heart accelerated as she turned to hear Derwent's decision. She did not know what she wanted him to say. To show Monstuart a lesson appealed strongly to her. To go to London and make her bows from Derwent's mansion, too, was a treat she craved. The Season was beginning—she would be there, at last. But on the other hand, she had a premonition that Monstuart would wreak a revenge of no small proportions. What could he do? "Always consider the worst alternative, and see if you could live with it," her father used to advise. Well, the worst Monstuart could do was keep Derwent's money from him for two years, and she could live with that. He couldn't have the marriage annulled. There were no possible grounds.

"Well, Derwent?" she asked.

Derwent didn't hear her. He sat with Melanie's white fingers curled up in his own while he smiled fondly on her. The decision was already made. "What?

84

Oh—yes, we shall do it, absolutely. And we shall have a great party in London, dear, to make up for the small wedding," he promised his blushing bride.

"Can you afford it?" Sally asked.

"It won't cost that much. Monstuart keeps a few servants at my house at Portman Place year-round. As to the expenses of running it, my hope was that you and Melanie's mama would stay with us in London and share expenses. In that manner, there is only one household to run. And it would only be for the Season. Afterwards, Melanie and I would go to Gravenhurst, and you would return to Ashford."

A whole Season in London! "Monstuart would particularly hate it," Sally pointed out. Her expression hovered between delight and chagrin.

"You said yourself you would pay no heed to him. It is the only way it can be accomplished. Naturally I will reimburse Mrs. Hermitage in two years," Derwent explained.

"You must say yes, Sally," Melanie begged. Tears pooled in her big blue eyes. "It won't be for long. Monstuart will *have* to give us money if we force his hand."

Forcing Monstuart's hand appealed strongly to Sally. The other three members of the group urged her to agree, and in the end she did, reluctantly.

The next twenty-four hours were a whirlwind of activity. There was the dash to the Bishop for a special license, to the local minister to make the arrangements; there were the wedding gowns to be enriched with new lace, a ring to be purchased, a footman sent off to London to ready the family mansion on Portman Square. There was a finer-than-usual meal to be ordered and arranged, and there was some secrecy to maintain through it all, for the town was not to be told till it was over. This last was Derwent's idea. "Just in case," as he ominously phrased it. His worry, obviously, was that Mrs. Colchester would write to Monstuart, and he would come bounding back to scotch the plan.

The small wedding took place without undue incident. The couple made their vows in the Hermitages' Rose Saloon, which was bedecked with many flowers for the occasion. Mrs. Hermitage wept copiously for joy, and Sally, too, felt tears welling up in her eyes. Melanie was a picture-book bride. Her sister wished she could capture the image by some magical means and hold it forever. It was impossible not to consider her own state of singleness and wonder if she would ever be standing before a minister, repeating those solemn vows. Twenty-one years old and not a sign of a suitor.

The arrangement was that the newlyweds would set straight off for London to take up residence in Derwent's house there, and the Hermitage ladies would join them in a week, allowing them that period of adjustment and honeymoon. It was not an idle week for Sally and her mother by any means. They had their toilette to attend to, as the London Season called for more elegance than even they possessed. It was Sally's hope to sublet the house during their absence, but this proved impossible on such short notice, and they hired an estate agent to do it for them after their remove. Throughout the seven days they were in considerable agitation, lest Monstuart come back. Mrs. Colchester and a few cronies were told of the wedding.

Monstuart did not come, but a letter from him

addressed to Derwent was sent down from the Col chester house and forwarded to London. Mrs. Hermitage was convinced it was a summons to go to DeBeirs, and was happy she had seen Melanie safely married before the missive should be read by Derwent. On the day of their departure, the post brought a brief note from Derwent, informing them to go to an address on Cavendish Square upon their arrival.

"What can this mean?" Mrs. Hermitage asked. "Are we not to stay with them at Portman Place?"

"It says we are to *join* them on Cavendish Square," Sally pointed out. "Perhaps his house is not ready, and some relative has lent them a place temporarily. Derwent is related to half of London. That must be it. No doubt we shall remove to Portman Place very soon."

In any case, the mansion before which their traveling carriage drew to a stop on Cavendish Square was an impressive edifice. Three stories of brick rose skyward, and the facade gleamed with dozens of windows. Everything about the house was of the first stare, from the high polish on the massive lion's-head brass knocker to the slate roof. Even the chimney pots glowed.

For Sally, it had felt like coming home to be driving once more through the bustling streets of London. She hadn't seen so many people for years and realized how very much she had missed dear, busy London. The awful feeling came over her that she had turned into a country mouse. A glance at the ladies' toilettes brought a stinging reminder of Monstuart's left-handed compliment on her coiffure *à la Grecque*. What fun to have a stylish hairdresser in to tend her locks.

With tears in her eyes, Melanie came pelting out the door of the mansion to embrace them. "Oh, Mama, Sally, I am so happy to see you. I never dreamed I would be so lonesome."

For half a heartbeat Sally feared the marriage was going poorly, but it was no such a thing. Melanie was the happiest of brides, lacking only her family to complete her bliss. Ronald—for Derwent was now called Ronald—was a paragon of a husband.

"He insisted on hiring this huge house when that horrid Monstuart rented our own out from under us, without even asking us," Melanie explained.

"You cannot mean it!" Her mother gasped. She was soon uttering further cries of outrage when Derwent rushed out to add his welcome.

"Not only did he rent the house on Portman Square; he is pocketing the money himself—putting it in my account, I mean, to pile up interest," Derwent said accusingly. "So I had to hire this one. I tremble to tell you what it is costing me, Mrs. Hermitage. I may have to borrow a little something from you before the Season is over."

"How much is the rent?" Sally asked with the direst forebodings.

"A thousand for the Season," he replied. "But with servants and so on, it will be more like twice that sum, for Monstuart saw fit to include my servants in the deal he made for letting my house out from under me."

"You have no idea how horrid he is," Melanie threw in.

"Does he know about the marriage, then?" Sally asked.

"Come inside and we shall tell you all about it," her sister said. The group hastened inside to hear the worst.

The interior of the mansion was every bit as fine as the exterior suggested. Sally could not but feel, when she looked at acres of marble hallway and molded ceilings, at a gilt-bannistered horseshoe stairway and a chandelier the size of a beech tree, that the four of them could have been comfortable with half the space, at half the price. They entered a palatial Gold Saloon, where they huddled together in one corner, feeling lost in space. A hundred guests would hardly have filled the area.

"Ronald wrote him the very day we arrived," Melanie replied, "and we have had an answer back today."

"Did he rent Derwent's house before he knew of the wedding?" Sally asked.

"Yes, months ago, and never telling Ronald. Imagine! His excuse was that he thought Ronald would put up with him while he was in London, as he did last year. You would think Ronald was a boy, to have these things kept from him—his own house."

"At least it was not revenge, then, as I feared," Sally said "What had he to say about the wedding?"

Melanie lifted her chin pugnaciously. "He ordered us to go to Gravenhurst, Ronald's country estate, if you please."

"Why would he do that?" Sally asked.

"Because that is the only place we can afford to

live without borrowing money from Mama. He refuses to give us so much as a farthing more than Ronald's bachelor allowance. It is all spite because of that DeBeirs girl."

"Is that what his letter was about?"

"The first one that he sent to Colchesters just told Ronald to join him at Chêne Baie, hoping he would eventually offer for Lady Mary, but after he learned we were married, he wrote the worst things, warning Ronald not to have you and Mama to live with us and that we are a very expensive brood and—everything. Oh, I hate him. I will not let him enter this house, and neither will Ronald. And that is why we are so glad you and Mama are here."

Sally felt weak with foreboding. "Perhaps he won't wish to enter," she said hopefully.

"Oh, yes, he is coming tomorrow morning, and you must handle him, Sally," Melanie told her.

"I wish you would not draw *me* into this any more than necessary."

"But it *is* necessary. *You* are the only one he listens to. You must make him give us some more money, for Ronald is at the bottom of his purse. In fact, we could only make a small deposit on the house rent, and you know you and I must be presented in the Queen's Drawing Room and have parties and pay for a box at the theater and—"

"We do sound rather an expensive brood, do we not?" Sally said weakly. She fell back against the brocade sofa. "It is for Derwent to discuss business matters with him, Melanie, not me."

"Ronald will dun him for the money, but you must soften him up."

"In that case, you had best let him into the house," Mrs. Hermitage advised.

"I mean we shall not see him socially, Mama," Melanie explained. "Though Ronald says he has wonderful parties and is excellent ton. He will—could introduce us to everyone, but he is so stubborn and ill-natured there is no counting on it. Oh, did I tell you? Ronald has got us a box on the grand tier at Drury Lane, and we are to attend the first play tomorrow night."

"How nice!" Mrs. Hermitage gushed.

Sally was pleased, too, but worries for the future cast a pall over her pleasure. She disliked to be always harping on money, but felt obliged to inquire, "How much did the box cost?"

"Only a hundred and fifty pounds for the whole season. Of course it is not paid for yet, but we can use it immediately," Melanie assured her. "And we are to have our presentation gowns made by Madame Laurier, Sally. Ronald's cousin, Lady Anglin, directed me to her. She is the best modiste in the whole city, but shockingly expensive. We shall go very soon to visit her. Ronald has already arranged to have our names submitted at St. James's."

As dinner was still a few hours away, some light refreshments were served to sustain the travelers. There was an excited hour of gossip and chatter, heavily sprinkled with the high cost of all the city's pleasures. But still, they did sound like delightful pleasures. Almost delightful enough to stay the pangs of apprehension that loomed at the edge of Sally's mind.

Dinner was such a grand affair that the whole twelve feet of the dining table was required to hold

91

all the silver dishes and crystal goblets and the massive floral arrangement that covered it. Four footmen served the party, at a cost to be determined at a later date, for Sally could not ask Derwent in front of the servants.

"It reminds me so very much of when your papa was alive," Mrs. Hermitage said, sighing wistfully. "How happy he would be to know his girls are to be presented. Melanie married, and now your turn is coming, Sal. There is no saying. Even you may nab someone in London."

Derwent, in an expansive mood, agreed. "Absolutely."

"We shall share our ball," Melanie decided. "I must take precedence, for I am married now—Lady Derwent. Are you not impressed?" she asked. "Before the Season is over, you will be married, too, Sally."

It was a happy thought to take up to bed, and a happy thought was needed to ward off the less-delightful worries of bills and Lord Monstuart's pending visit.

Chapter Eight

Knowing Lord Monstuart's penchant for early arrivals, Miss Hermitage was up by eight the next morning to make a careful toilette. The sprigged or mulled muslins that suited Ashford were not fine enough for London. She chose a gold lutestring, narrowly striped in emerald green and finished with matching bindings. Bows and lace were eschewed. A more severe elegance suited her years and sophistication. Her only ornaments were a small golden locket and the emerald ring she always wore.

By nine o'clock she had breakfasted alone and begun a tour of the downstairs. She discovered the ballroom, an enormous chamber of barnlike proportions and palatial appointments. She had soon peopled it in imagination with waltzing ladies and handsome gentlemen. There was a heady excitement reeling in her, an impatience to get out into the city to enjoy all the frivolities from which she had been so long barred. London was her native habitat. No feeling of strangeness came to lessen her eagerness. And this evening they would be at the theater!

But first she must meet Monstuart. She wished the others would come down yet felt some contrary emotion when they did so before his arrival. Setting his clock to city hours, Monstuart did not call till eleven, by which time the whole group was in a state of fidget with waiting and worrying. So much depended on his reaction to the wedding.

Monstuart was quite simply furious. He couldn't forbid the match outright, and to try would only have lent it an irresistible hue of melodrama. He had hoped that familiarity with the Hermitages would open Derwent's eyes, but he had obviously underestimated Miss Hermitage. That vixen—he should have known she wouldn't be content with her provincial invalid. She had engineered this match for her own advantage. He was afraid what he might do if she was smiling triumphantly, so he ignored her as long as possible.

The first omens, upon his arrival, seemed good. He came in smiling to congratulate his nephew and wish the bride happy. The visitors received a curt bow, and a brief "Good morning, ladies," which was better than Sally expected. As she saw only the back of his head for the next several minutes, it was difficult to gauge his temper. The fact that he carried a gift for the bride seemed hopeful. It was a small package containing a ring with a row of four precious stones across the top. "Sapphires and diamonds, to match your eyes and your smile respectively," he said when she opened it.

His next speech was less encouraging. "Of course, you will not have much opportunity to show it off this year, at Gravenhurst. I assume you will be removing there directly, as your town house is rented, Derwent." A steely eye was directed at his nephew as he spoke. "As soon as the bride's family have terminated their brief visit, that is to say." His black head turned toward the visiting ladies, and their hearts clenched.

Sally felt her insides quake at the venom in that glance. Her mother said, "Oh, my dear!" in a falling voice while her shoulders slumped.

Any show of weakness was anathema to Sally. She stiffened her spine for combat. "Yes, the house is only rented for two months. After that the newlyweds will be going to Gravenhurst, and we will return to Ashford."

Monstuart felt a ripple of rage scamper up his spine at her bold attitude. He hadn't a doubt in the world that she was the prime mover in this affair. The rest of them rolled together hadn't the gumption to cross him. He crossed his arms, leaned back in a bellicose manner, and counted to ten quietly to himself. "You are taking advantage of this opportunity to make your bows, are you, Miss Hermitage?"

She nodded. "As you suggested I should do, milord. You were quite right. We are all looking forward to attending Drury Lane this evening, as well."

Monstuart's dark gaze flickered to his nephew. "I hope you have had the foresight to book a box for the night, Derwent, or the ladies will find themselves on the outside, looking in."

"Ronald is not so remiss as you imagine," Sally said. Derwent's Christian name came without thinking, from some instinctive knowledge that her using it would annoy the uncle. "He has taken a box for the Season."

One would not have thought it possible for Monstuart's back to become any straighter. It was more a convulsion than a straightening that occurred as he directed a glare at Derwent, who blanched visibly under that unflinching stare. "May your guardian inquire what you are using for blunt? This pretentious and unnecessarily large mansion must have pretty well cleaned you out."

Derwent gulped and charged in. "I want to talk to you about that, Monty. Now that I have a wife to keep . . ."

"And the wife's family," Monstuart added without bothering to glance at them.

"Yes, well, you know what I mean. You rented *my* house. We must live somewhere."

"I strongly advise you remove to Gravenhurst. It is the only spot you can afford."

"Deuce take it, I have fifteen thousand a year!"

Monstuart's jaws worked with the effort of keeping his temper in check. "No, Cawker, you have two thousand a year, till I decide you are capable of handling more. I see no signs of it at the present. I know you had run through the half of that sum before ever coming here. Don't think I mean to turn your fortune over to you to be squandered by your relatives. Till you show some signs of maturity, I keep a tight rein on the purse."

Derwent blustered up ineffectively. "If getting married don't show signs of maturity, I should like to know what does!"

Monstuart caught a glimmer of amusement in

Miss Hermitage's green eyes, and the last vestige of his control fled. "Maturity! I've seen more signs of it in a puppy! Sneaking off behind my back like an adolescent miscreant for a hole-in-the-wall wedding engineered by a scheming hussy—"

Derwent was on his feet, turning an astonishing shade of red. "You will answer for that, sir! I will not sit here and have my wife traduced in my own house."

"Lord Melbrook's house. Yours is rented. And I did not refer to your wife," he added with a scathing glare at the wife's sister.

Sally was the next one to jump to her feet. Her eyes glittered dangerously, and her voice was trembling with fury. "I suggest you take your leave now, Monstuart, before this degenerates into a physical brawl." Her hands clenched into fists from the effort not to slap that arrogant, hateful face. "You have done what you came to do—namely insult me and confirm your intention of keeping Derwent's money from him. You've done your worst."

"That's what you think!" His voice cut like a knife, and his eyes blazed. "If you want to play rough, I can, and shall, do considerably more. I can make this town so hot you'll wish you'd never got your talons into this simpleton of a boy and schemed your way to London."

"Here we feared you meant to show us a cold shoulder!" she said with an arch laugh to her cohorts, who stared in horror at the awful turn the meeting had taken.

Monstuart looked around the group with an air of loathing. He saw his nephew surrounded by a parcel of expensive ladies, whom he was now convinced were out to fleece the boy. His anger was the fiercer for being partly directed at himself. He had been negligent to leave the lad unattended.

"Just what do you hope to accomplish by this?" he asked Sally.

She tossed her shoulders insouciantly. "I hope to garner some of those joys you constantly reminded me of at Ashford. Why, it was you who put the idea of coming to London in my head."

"I think not. You came in hope of making a good match. Let me disabuse you of so foolish a notion. Gentlemen do not marry dowerless women."

"Lord Derwent did," she pointed out, blinking her eyes in a parody of beguiled innocence. "Surely you are not suggesting that your nephew is not a gentleman!"

"See here, Monty," Derwent began in a cajoling tone, "the thing's done, and there's no point being stubborn about it. It will only make it worse if you cut up stiff. I mean to say, we shall be meeting every second day in society, and if you are planning to cast slurs on us . . ."

"Do be reasonable, Lord Monstuart," Sally added in a sneering way. "You must see I am at disadvantage enough without a dowry. How shall I ever snare myself a rich husband if you give me the reputation of being a managing female as well? Why, your nephew will have Mama and me around his neck *forever* if you have your way."

"That is all that saves you from being publicly exposed for the adventuress you are," he told her. He rose stiffly and looked down his nose at her. "Go ahead. Do your worst, Miss Hermitage. You will not do it with my nephew's money. Nor will you find many gentlemen so gullible and easily led as this Johnnie Raw."

"I do not look for *many*, milord. One is all I require. I have no inclination for bigamy, I promise you. I leave the shadier vices to the royal family."

"Let me give you a tip, miss. Pert country manners will cut no ice in society. It if is your intention to pass yourself off as a well-bred lady, you should learn to curb that sharp tongue."

"I can pass myself off as a polite simpleton as well as the next lady—provided I am not goaded beyond endurance by any ill-mannered person. You are leaving?" she asked as he directed a fulminating stare on her before turning away. "We enjoyed your little visit, Lord Monstuart. Do come back soon. *Au revoir.*"

As the door was closed by the butler, Monstuart hadn't even the pleasure of slamming it behind him. He wreaked his temper on his curled beaver instead, as he poked it on to his head with a vicious stab. There was a thundering silence in the ornate Gold Saloon when he was gone.

"Can he really keep your money?" Melanie asked her husband in a frightened whisper.

"Of course he can. He is the sole executor of my father's will. He can do whatever he wants."

Sally punched a pretty green satin cushion in frustration. "I wish Papa were here. *He* would find some legal way out of this impossible situation."

A soft smile turned up the corner of Mrs. Hermitage's lips, and she said softly, "Sir Darrow Willowby!"

Sally frowned at the name, which disturbed an echo from the past. "What did you say, Mama?"

"Sir Darrow Willowby! The man who was Papa's partner the last few years he was working, my dear."

"Your old flirt!"

"Not at all, but he was as shrewd as can hold together. If anything can be done, he is the very one to do it. I meant to be in touch with him in any case. I shall send him a note this very day. This very instant!" she said, rising to search the cavernous building for a study.

Her elder daughter hurried after her. "Do you think it wise to publicize our predicament, Mama? We always said that in the worst case we would spend our own money to tide us over. I an not eager for the straits we are in to be discussed in every drawing room.

"Pshaw. Sir Darrow won't tell anyone. He is close as a clock. It is required in his profession, for those lawyers hear all manner of disgraceful things about their clients. A little bankruptcy is not worth mentioning to them."

"Caution him not to tell his wife. Ladies are not so close."

"I don't know that he has a wife, Sal. She was ill at the time he joined your father. He might be a widower by now. I think I heard he is, in fact. I'll ask him to come around here. I could not face going to your father's office. The memories would overcome me, and it is so unflattering to be seen with red eyes."

Lord and Lady Derwent absented themselves to call on various relatives of the groom after luncheon, but Sally elected to remain home with her mother to speak to Sir Darrow Willowby, whom she remembered fondly from her youth. She did not remember him being quite so old, nor so diminutive, as he turned out to be. He was not a day under sixty, with already a slight stooping forward around the shoulders. He wore his snow-white hair parted in the center, to lengthen even further his pencil-thin face. But the eyes were still a bright and mischievous blue, with the brows sprouting in thicker strands than before.

"Ho, Mrs. Hermitage—Mabel, you haven't changed one iota since I saw you last," he shouted from the doorway of the saloon. Soon he was shuffling in, smiling at them both. "You never mean to tell me you still have this minx on your hands?" he asked in surprise as he looked at Sally. "I made sure she'd be married from the schoolroom. The prettiest face in London—present company, of course, excepted," he added with a bow to the beaming mother.

"Darrow! How nice it is to see you again. Just like old times," the hostess declared. Tears sprung to her eyes at the memories inevitably evoked by this vision from the past.

"You would have seen me long since, had you let me know where you were living, shatterbrain," he scolded, shaking a finger at her. "I told you to keep in touch, and how many years have passed? Never mind I don't want to know. It is too many."

He sat down, placed his cane between his knees, and rubbed his hands together. Then he assumed a more serious aspect and said, "Now, dry those tears and let us hear what hobble you have fallen into, Mabel. You know I am never savage with you."

Mrs. Hermitage outlined, with many polite cir-

101

cumlocutions, her situation, bringing him up to date with the marriage of her younger daughter.

Sir Darrow listened sharply. "Why, you are well off and don't know it. Half the lords in London couldn't pay their bills if everything they owned were sold off at auction. And you have nabbed an earl for one of the girls into the bargain. You'll have no trouble disposing of this saucy piece," he added with an admiring study of Sally. "Should have brought her out two or three years ago. I have been waiting that long to make her an offer. Ha-ha." He finished with a waggish shake of his white head to show his jest.

"What we really want to know, Darrow, is whether Monstuart can keep Derwent's money from him for the two years, as he threatens to do," Mrs. Hermitage explained.

Sir Darrow raised his brows and pursed his lips in a well-remembered fashion that gave him a comical air. "In a word, yes. Legally, he can. Speaking more practically, he will look a flaming jackass if he does. There is not point in it. The cent percenters will be happy to get their hooks into young Derwent. They will lend him any amount, with an income of fifteen thousand behind him. I cannot imagine for a moment Monstuart would be so woolly-headed. What has got him into this pucker, eh? This minx is giving him a hard time, I warrant," he ventured, looking at Sally. "She is very much in his style, if I am not mistaken."

"Well, you are mistaken, Darrow, for they never meet but they come to cuffs," Mrs. Hermitage informed him.

"He is a trifle high-handed. I never had much to

do with him myself; your husband, of course, handled the Monstuart case. He don't like being crossed, if I remember the story aright."

Sally's interest perked up immediately. "What case did Papa handle for him?" she asked.

"One of those delicate affairs never spoken of in front of young ladies," he replied. "A paternity suit, was it? No, not quite that simple. Crim. con., perhaps. Something in the petticoat line. I can look it up and let you know if you have a mind to tease him, but don't breathe a word of how you found out."

"I would appreciate learning all the details," Sally answered with a quiet, anticipatory smile lurking in the depths of her eyes. "And the sooner, the better."

"Must not bruit it about town, but I don't have to tell the Hermit's daughter that. Use it to trim him into line, if you like. No harm in that. So, Mabel," he continued, "you have outrun the grocer again. If you need funds, I can advance you something till next quarter or till Derwent comes into his own. There is no hurry about repaying. Your husband's business has done me proud. I learned a few sly tricks from the Hermit, and it keeps folks coming to me. I ain't as sharp as your husband, but I am sharper than any other shyster in town, if I do say so myself."

"We could not take money from you, Darrow," she answered, but without that conviction that a determined negative would have carried.

It was for Sally to refuse with equal politeness and a good deal more firmness.

"This one rules the roost, I see," he said to her

mother. "Does she lead you a merry chase, Mabel? Her papa often forecast it. He warned you times out of mind to get her shackled to the first decent fellow who offered. I am amazed she is still on the shelf. Ha, the London beaux will soon take care of that. That is why you are here, I daresay?" he asked, turning to Sally.

"You read me like an open book, Sir Darrow. Have you any eligible partis to put forward?"

"My set would all be too old for you, my girl. I run with Prinny's pack these days. A ripe bunch for plucking, you must know. I'll keep my eyes open. I'll have Prinny invite you to one of his larger dos at Carlton House and let you look over the Season's offerings. Stay away from Walworth and Kidder. Libertines and wastrels, with not a sou to their names."

Sally made a mental note of the names, and soon Sir Darrow picked up his cane in preparation of leaving. "I am working up a brief for Lord Handworth. He wants to dump his wife, but you must not say I told you so. I shall toddle along now and be in touch soon. Good day, Mabel. You are as pretty as ever. Perhaps we shall get shackled, eh? Ha-ha."

"Is Lady Willowby—"

"She passed on a few years ago." He shook his head as he hobbled from the room.

"Don't forget to let me know what matter it was Papa handled for Lord Monstuart," Sally called after him.

"Ho, you are determined to get the upper hand with him, I see. I'll do what I can to help you. Least I can do for the Hermit. Good day, ladies."

"Well, that is that," Mrs. Hermitage said when they were alone once more. "Monstuart need not give us any money if he chooses. I might as well be in touch with our man of business and see about selling those Consols. I hate to do it."

"Sell a thousand pounds' worth," Sally suggested. "The opera box must be paid for, and we'll need some operating money."

It was hard to dip into their little fund, but when Melanie and Derwent came home with invitations to not less than two rout parties and one ball, when there was the box at the theater waiting to be occupied that same evening, it was impossible not to be more excited than worried.

And it was, indeed, an evening to remember. It seemed that all of the ten thousand had come to Drury Lane, wearing their finest diamonds and their gayest smiles. Lord Derwent had many friends who wished to meet his new bride and bid her happy. A new pair of beauties in town, one blond, the other a striking brunette, were bound to garner their fair share of attention. Sally noticed with satisfaction that they had the fullest box in the house during the first intermission.

But the highlight of the evening occurred during the second intermission. Sir Darrow's white head peeped into the box, eyes dancing merrily. "Mabel, ladies, put on your best smiles. There is someone who wants you to come to his box for wine."

For no sane reason, Sally found herself thinking the "someone" was Monstuart. How like his arrogance, to command that they go to his box. "Pray request 'someone' to come to our box if he wishes to meet us." She smiled.

"We'll never get him squeezed through the portal before the intermission is over. It took a brace of us to get him in," Sir Darrow replied.

Such a portly gentleman was obviously not Monstuart. It was Mrs. Hermitage who uttered a squeal of delight. "Not Prinny, Darrow!"

"No less. Come along, or he'll have drunk up all the wine."

The ladies were not tardy to nip along to the most famous box in the house. Physically, the visit was an extremely uncomfortable squeeze, but it set the cap on their evening. His Royal Hugeness, as the Prince of Wales was being called that week, found the daughters comely. Their older and more fully figured mother, a dame in Prinny's preferred style, was pronounced an Incomparable.

It was generally agreed among the ladies later that Monstuart's threat of ostracization might very well be overcome. He did not attend the play, but Sally found her mind veering often in his direction. She wondered what "delicate matter" it was her father had handled for him and how soon she might have the opportunity of throwing it in his face.

Chapter Nine

A Season of six weeks is not very long when it has to include a presentation at Court, an introduction to polite society, the setting up of a court of admirers, the singling out of one of them as the one to be attached, and the final landing of him in her net. Without ever wasting a minute, Sally didn't see how she was to pull the thing off. The gentlemen she wished to draw to her saloon were elusive. Derwent's friends, all callow youths, were arriving in abundance. They were amusing rattles to have dance attendance on her at parties, but there was not one in the lot she could envisage spending an evening alone with in anything but absolute boredom. The other alternative was the aging cronies of Sir Darrow Willowby and her late papa, who were always attentive. Sir Darrow was the Hermitages' usual escort to all the ton functions.

Shortly after the ladies were anointed with respectability at Queen Charlotte's Drawing Room, Sir Darrow arranged for the family to attend one of Prinny's fabulous parties at Carlton House. This do required three new gowns of an elegance nearly matching the presentation gowns. "For we do not want to show the world we've been rusticating all these years," Mrs. Hermitage pointed out. "Do you think the ecru crepe does anything for me, Sal? I fear it is a poor choice. It is the same faded shade as my face. I must use more rouge. We antiques are all resorting to it to lend us a touch of color."

Now a happy matron, Melanie could put off the white of maidenhood and had concocted an ice-blue peau de soie gown that made her look even younger than her eighteen years. It rankled a little with Sally that she must still wear white, when she was three years older, but the color was not downright unbecoming. As Sir Darrow had the wits to supply a corsage of red flowers, she did not look quite as though she were masquerading as a youngster.

"I do hope Monstuart will not be there," Mrs. Hermitage fretted. "Do you suppose it is *his* doing that none of the fellows the proper age are calling on you, Sal? He has a wide circle of friends, the very gentlemen who ought to be courting you."

"I wouldn't put it a bit past him," Sally replied with an angry jerk at her gloves.

"Do be careful, dear. The kidskin splits if you look too hard at it. I have gone through three pairs of gloves this Season, and it is early times yet. They cost a fortune, too."

"How is the thousand pounds you converted from Consols holding out?" Sally asked.

Her mother blinked in surprise. "Why, it is gone long ago. I have had to draw out two thousand more since then."

"We must cut back," Sally scolded, but in her heart she knew it could not be done. She had no more desire than her family to appear in anything but the highest kick of fashion. Another thousand would have to be taken out for their ball, but she meant to draw the line absolutely at five thousand. That would leave them ten thousand for the next two years, if Monstuart could not be brought to heel. And really, he was so remarkably stubborn it was a genuine possibility. He had never called in three weeks since his first visit and scarcely acknowledged that he knew them when they met in society.

They were interrupted by the sound of the door knocker. "That will be Darrow." Mrs. Hermitage smiled.

He was soon shown in. "How are my two girl-friends?" he asked. His blue eyes turned first to the mother for a close scrutiny, then to Sally. "Six of one and half a dozen of the other," he concluded. "I cannot decide which is the more lovely. But I know which one Prince George will favor. He has no use for young fillies. Are the Derwents not coming with us?"

"They went on ahead in Ronald's carriage," Mrs. Hermitage replied. "Five in yours would be crowded, Darrow. We do not want to arrive crushed."

"Ho, you'll be squeezed to death once you get there. Prinny has five hundred coming for an intimate little evening. Let us all cross our fingers and pray he don't decide to play his flute for us. Poor boy, he has no idea how ridiculous he looks and how badly he plays. His squawking reminds me of the sounds coming from an abattoir."

"You didn't hear whether Monstuart is attending?" Mrs. Hermitage asked.

"He is one of the ten thousand, but whether he is one of the five hundred awaits to be seen. I did not forget your commission to me regarding him," he added, turning to Sally.

"The case Papa handled for him?"

"Exactly. I must report total failure. The file was removed from the office. Your papa sometimes did so at a client's special request. The bill is on the books—five hundred guineas. That indicates a substantial case, but the exact nature of it remains a mystery, except that I recall it involved a light-skirt. Well, are we off?"

Excitement at the approaching party diluted the disappointment of not learning Monstuart's wicked past. He was so seldom met, in any case, that there was little likelihood of being able to twit him about it.

The entrance hall of Carlton House was lit with hundreds of lamps, giving the effect of stepping from night into the blazing heat of day. The heat was even worse than the light. The gentlemen, who were required by decency to keep their coats on their shoulders, thought so, at least. They tugged surreptitiously at their cravats, gasping for air. The Prince found the room comfortable, despite the heavily ornamented uniform he wore.

"The on dit is that the jacket weighs what it cost—two hundred pounds," Sir Darrow chuckled. "We are in luck tonight. He don't play the flute when he's decked out in his comic opera uniform. Here he comes now, to do the pretty. Butter him up, ladies, and he'll make you both duchesses."

The Prince Regent was in high spirits. He had just that day learned he had lost two pounds. "High time you came out of the woodwork, Madam, and let society admire your charming daughters," he told Mrs. Hermitage. "I attended the Queen's Drawing Room and saw your gels make their bows. The prettiest pair in the lineup, and the three loveliest ladies in town, I might add. I see from the corner of Willowby's mouth that he is not pleased with me. Poaching, eh what, Willowby? He'll take me to court, heh-heh."

The ladies curtsied, so awed by all the magisterial splendor of house and uniform that they scarcely heard the inanities flowing from his lips.

"There is a bit of a dance going forth in the next room," the Prince told Sally. "I would ask you to waltz, but the old quizzes at Almack's would frown at me. No good making those charming eyes at me, lass. My authority stops at the doors of Almack's. The patronesses reign there. Be civil to Countess Lieven, and she will give you the nod. I'll introduce you now."

He turned aside to speak to a gaunt female wearing the strangest hair style ever seen in public. It looked as though she had starched her hair and gotten caught in a violent windstorm, to stiffen it into spikes. The Russian ambassador's wife was one of the all-powerful patronesses of Almack's club, however, and was catered to by everyone. Even the Prince gave her a great smacking kiss on the cheek and called her "My dear Dorothea."

"So this is the Hermit's daughter," Countess Lieven said, skimming her eyes over the new beauty. "You didn't get your looks from your papa, did you? I hope you nicked a corner of his brains. I adored him. We must have a chat later. I am on my way to the table before the salmon and daubed goose are all gone. What a wretched little snipe that was you served for dinner, Your Majesty. Since you are gone on a diet, we are all starving to death. No jellies or creams for dessert. You know I detest fruit—slow poison. Delighted to have met you, Miss Hermitage."

She was off to the table, and Sir Darrow led the ladies through various chambers to goggle at the ornate decor till their eyes ached. "I should have brought my smoked glasses," Sir Darrow complained. "The lights here give me the migraine. Ah, here is an excellent chap, Wilton Parkes. He will make you a good partner while your mother and I escape to the card room, Sally."

Their ideas of a good partner did not jibe. Sally could not feel a gentleman on the windy side of forty was entirely agreeable, but the escorts Sir Darrow supplied were never young. She endured half an hour of slightly archaic chivalry from Parkes while scanning the room for more youthful companionship.

She noticed Monstuart had entered during the dance and taken up a position at the side of the room. She thought he might come forward at the set's end, but he chose another lady. Parkes, fatigued after the unusual exertion of the cotillion, gratefully handed Miss Hermitage over to a confrere, Mr. Peacock.

Outside of Monstuart, Peacock was the youngest man in the room, though he was about twice Melanie's age. Unlike Sir Darrow and Parkes, he was conversable. He had that facility to remain interested and interesting past his prime. As he had made a point to be presented to Sally, he was regarded with some favor by her.

"At last," he said with a languishing sigh when he offered her his arm. The laughter lurking in his eyes robbed the words of folly.

She looked with rising interest to gauge his appearance at close range. He smiled, showing a rather dashing face that was not far from reckless. "You are a difficult young lady to meet, Miss Hermitage. I have been staring at you through my opera glasses at the theater, my quizzing glass at the routs, my carriage window in the park, and my own unaided orbs at balls for close on two weeks now, trying to catch your attention. I expect you have been ignoring me to pique my interest."

"I assure you I never saw you before this evening, sir. Odd you have not had yourself presented before now. Shyness, obviously, is not at the root of it."

"Bashfulness is for boys. The fact is I don't run with Derwent and those juveniles who surround you. I knew sooner or later you would find your proper milieu, the Prince Regent's set."

"That's hard to take as a compliment! The ladies of his set are no longer in the first blush of youth. If you will look, Mr. Peacock, you will see I am wearing a white gown."

"I never judge a book by its cover. I have done more than stare at you. I have also hung about at your elbow, and I know your conversation is more interesting than your puppies deserve."

She smiled, pleased with his flattery. "It's

strange I never noticed you before if you have been underfoot these two weeks."

"I have often observed you never look *down*, Miss Hermitage. You hold your head so high you only see gentlemen seven feet or taller. Underfoot was the wrong place for me to hang about. I would have done better to hang from a tree branch in the park."

"Except that you might have been taken for a monkey."

"*Mis*taken, surely!" he objected with a readiness of wit that was welcome after Mr. Parke's staid common sense. "You have a radiant smile, you know. It beams like the sun. I wish you would stop. We don't need any more heat or light in here."

"I thought monkeys enjoyed a warm climate."

"We are going to get along just fine, Miss Hermitage," he decided. He tucked her hand under his elbow and led her to the floor when Fate, with her natural perversity, promptly struck up a waltz. The waltz was not permitted for debs till the Patronesses of Almack's decided they were sufficiently bronzed to withstand its insidious temptation.

Peacock led Sally out for a glass of wine instead. With a parting glance over her shoulder, she saw Monstuart looking after her, frowning even while he whirled his partner around the floor. Mr. Peacock was subjected to a few jibes at his fine jacket and exquisite cravat when it occurred to his partner that his name must not escape unchallenged.

"You wear a less appropriate name," he retorted. "I find it hard to believe a family of hermits brought forth such a dazzler. In fact, to speak of hermits bringing forth anything but philosophy refutes their calling. We must discuss this mystery further.

I'll call on you tomorrow afternoon and take you to Hyde Park. We'll select my tree, and next time you are there you can bring me a fruit."

"And a chain to put around your neck. If you are to be my pet, you must become accustomed to the leash."

"I cannot promise such docility, even for the Hermitess," he answered with one of his reckless smiles that sent her heart racing faster. "I misread your character if you would be happy with a tame pet on a string. No shackles for me. I'm not interested in marriage." He looked a challenge at her.

"You misunderstood me, sir. It is not my intention to marry my pet. Ladies hardly ever do, do they?"

"I've seen more than one marry a puppy, or even a jackass, but I take your point. Is it possible I've met my match?" His bold eyes raked her from head to toe in a way that made her feel naked. His eyes flickered to the door, and he added, "I fear I have. It is Monstuart, come to rescue you from my clutches. He will give you a stern lecture on my lack of character. Pay him no heed. I'm not nearly so bad as I let on. Oh, about Hyde Park ... shall we say three tomorrow?"

With Monstuart pacing quicking toward her, she said in a loud voice, "Three o'clock is fine, Mr. Peacock. I look forward to it." Mr. Peacock bowed and aimed a laughing bow at Monstuart as he departed.

"I might have known!" was Monstuart's first speech, said in a loud, angry voice.

"Good evening, Monstuart. Come to read me a lecture? It is not necessary. Mr. Peacock has already told me he has no character. When a gentleman has such a ready tongue and pleasing wit, however, it can be overlooked. One can't have everything."

"I doubt it's his pleasing appearance that drew you to him."

"The attraction was initially on the gentleman's part. I confess I find him amusing. You imply it is his lack of character that draws me?"

"No, Miss Hermitage, I acquit you of any girlish sentiment in your affairs. My implication is that it is his fortune that appeals to you."

A bright smile beamed. "What delightful news you bring. So unlike you! I made sure the man was a pauper. The interesting ones usually are. Who would have expected an eligible parti to be so charming?"

"He is not eligible."

"Now, that is more the sort of thing I expected to hear from you. You have come to tell me he is married, with a dozen children. He beats his wife and starves the children."

"The man is a bachelor, so far as I know."

Sally cast a laughing look at him. "You're slipping, Lord Monstuart."

"The word eligible has a dual connotation. It includes decent birth, along with fortune. You must not let your interest in the latter blind you to propriety."

Her eyes snapped at this thrust, but she refused to argue in public. "Peacock is a good old name."

"That's probably why he borrowed it."

"You mean it is not his *real* name?" she asked, more intrigued than dismayed.

"He says himself he only took it for a jest. He

came sailing home from India a month ago with a fortune in his pockets. Some part of it, I hear, was made from the opium trade with China. As for the rest of it, it is as shady as his parentage."

Sally was shocked to hear it but assumed a bland face. "It is odd one should meet him in the home of the First Gentleman of Europe, is it not?"

"It is exactly where I would have expected to meet him. Money is the requirement to sit down to cards with the Prince's set. Once a man has a pocketful of his chits, invitations to such dos as this have a way of popping up in the post. You have made an engagement with Peacock?"

"What big ears you have, Lord Monstuart. Yes, we are going out tomorrow."

"I would not repeat the outing, if I were you."

"We shall see," she replied, looking about the room in a way that clearly finished the topic.

A flush of color stained Monstuart's swarthy cheeks. "You came here to make a profitable match," he said. "Peacock is not your man. He would no more marry you than he'd give up gambling. You won't find him nearly so biddable as Derwent." The look Sally directed at him would have shriveled a bowl of greens, but Monstuart remained unwilted. "Stick to your callow youths, still wet behind the ears. You will find them easier to lead."

"Don't underestimate me, Monstuart. Peacock is not unobtainable. He has plenty of money, which is *of course* the only thing of interest to me. I can supply the breeding and connections. At least we shan't be dull."

"Nor even respectable, for very long."

A flash of green fire lit her eyes. "An odd subject for you to choose, milord. How respectable would *you* be if my father hadn't pulled you out of the suds?" Monstuart gave a conscious start. "Have I caught you off guard? Don't worry. Your five hundred guineas bought the family's silence. We would not dream of betraying your little lapse from respectability, and as Lady Dennison appears to be remaining in the country, you might *pass* for a gentleman of character. If you can restrain yourself from any further unwise impulses, that is to say. The Hermit is no longer here to protect you."

Monstuart's nostrils quivered in outrage. "I can't imagine what Willowby is about, bringing you to this place."

"I am inclined to agree with you. I haven't met a single gentleman who is completely respectable." Her skimming gaze included the present company.

He ignored the taunt. After a few moments' silent sipping of champagne, he continued in a calmer tone. "How are the finances coming along? Have you outrun the grocer yet?"

"I only spend the money, I am not the accountant. Ask your nephew. When the keeper of Debtors' Prison comes after us, Derwent is the one they'll carry away."

"He knows where to find me," Monstuart said. "Would you care to stand up for a dance, Miss Hermitage?"

"No, thank you. I am going into the refreshment parlor—to save on groceries at home, you know. Every little bit helps."

"Some restraint in personal adornment would

118

help even more," he pointed out as his eyes ran over her white gown.

Sally was secure that he would find no flaws. "Oh, but I most particularly promised you I would update my toilette, when you urged me to at Ashford."

A reluctant smile tugged at his lips. "Are you enjoying your Season?"

"Not much, till this evening. But I think now things are taking a turn for the better," she told him with a smile that was a shade too demure to trust.

"That compliment does not refer to your present partner, I think."

"You *are* clever."

"You've been warned. I'll say no more on the subject of Peacock."

"Good. I am relieved you don't mean to become repetitive. A word to the wise is always considered sufficient."

Sally looked about for Peacock after Monstuart left her. She knew that some of the gentlemen had retired to a parlor for cards, and as he was not to be found, she assumed he had joined them.

As the family went home, she said to Willowby, "What do you know about a man called Peacock, who was there tonight?"

"An amusing rascal. Well inlaid, but he flies too high for you, Sally. Stick to your own sort."

"I stood up with him. He seems to think I may be his sort."

"Ho, get a promise from him in writing before you throw your heart at that one. If you can get it in writing, I'll hold him to it. Never worry about that. I know my way around a contract as well as anyone. Wretched meal, was it not?" he asked, turning to Mrs. Hermitage.

"Who could eat in that heat and glare?"

"No braised capon, no savory pies. I didn't see an edible sweet on the table. It is always like that when Prinny goes on one of his demmed diets. Then he has Carème bring a tray to his room before he retires. He served us cold sandwiches and water at Brighton last month. If he don't smarten up his table, he will be dining alone. Reminds me, I am taking you all to dinner at the Clarendon after that do at Almack's on Thursday. You are going to Almack's, I trust?"

"Countess Lieven has promised vouchers," Mrs. Hermitage was happy to inform him.

"You won't find the likes of Peacock there," Willowby told Sally. "The other lad, Parkes—he is the young fellow for you."

Sally had no intention of pursuing "young" Mr. Parkes, but began to realize Mr. Peacock was not quite the thing. A date for the outing to the Park was already made and would be kept, but she would not go out with him again.

Chapter Ten

A drive in the park with Mr. Peacock proved amusing. His conversation was more frivolous than intellectual, but his carriage was the finest to be seen and his team of matched grays above reproach. To add a touch of respectability to the outing, Sally arranged to meet her sister and Derwent there and walk around the grounds with them. She was worried to see how well Derwent and Peacock got on together. Before they had gone ten yards, the ladies fell behind while the men set a brisker pace ahead.

Mellie soon wanted to rest on a bench, and the men disappeared from view. When they returned, there was talk of the four of them going "on the town" that evening.

"We are to go to Almack's, Ronald," Melanie reminded him.

"That dull place? Peacock says we'll have a livelier time at the Pantheon masquerade."

"It has all been arranged," Sally said, and considered the matter closed.

"We must drop in and say how do you do," Ron-

121

ald agreed. "That is no reason we must stay all night. We'll get together later, Peacock, around eleven."

But things were not really lively at Almack's before eleven. "I shan't be leaving Almack's," Sally said firmly.

Peacock regarded her with a laughing eye. He was not the sort to be put off with a little reluctance. "I'll bring along an extra domino, in case you change your mind. I highly recommend a lady employ all her prerogatives, and changing her mind is one of the most common."

His persistence began to seem ill-bred to Miss Hermitage, and she decided to give him a set-down. "Saying no is also a prerogative—one that a gentleman accepts without argument, Mr. Peacock."

"That depends on the gentleman," he parried, still in good humor. "I accept your refusal—for now. But another time—a picnic to Richmond Park, perhaps."

Ronald gave his tentative agreement, but no firm plan was made. Sally and Melanie soon asked to be taken home. They wanted to make a careful toilette for their important first visit to Almack's.

King Street was lined with carriages disgorging passengers when they arrived at the club. Sally found herself scanning the row of vehicles in vain for Monstuart's. A maximum of seventeen hundred of the ten thousand could be accommodated at the club at one time, and nearly that number appeared to be present when they entered. It took her all of two minutes to find her quarry, halfway down the one-hundred-foot ballroom. One black jacket looked much like another, but as he happened to be looking toward the entrance, she recognized him.

Monstuart nodded briefly, then turned his shoulder and continued talking to his partner. His cool behavior put Sally in a bad mood before she ever stood up to dance. The evening at Almack's established the Hermitage ladies as being accepted by the ton without adding much to their pleasure. Mrs. Hermitage had the best time of them all. She was singled out for a brief flirtation with the Prince Regent, who told her, and several other matrons, he had only come for a cose with them. Melanie could not be entirely happy when Derwent checked his watch every quarter hour and asked if they could leave now.

For Sally, the party was much like any other. She was besieged by young puppies and Sir Darrow's cronies, while gentlemen of the right age and station in life looked at her from the sidelines. She felt in her bones it was Monstuart who deflected their advances. He was among them and could have introduced her to any number of partis, but he did nothing of the sort.

She took the idea he was even disparaging her in some manner. Soon she had evidence of it. Silence Jersey, another of the patronesses, led a new gentleman forward to make her acquaintance. He was one of Monstuart's set who decided to break ranks.

"This fellow has hounded me to death to be presented to you," she said. Her bright eyes darted between them, curious to see if she was arranging a possible match. "He has done nothing but harass me since he got here. He finally found the way to cajole me; he has promised to invite me to his next houseparty. Sir Giles's parties are top of the trees, Miss Hermitage. At Stonecroft, you must know, his estate in Hampshire. He breeds ponies, and tells me you are the likeliest filly he has seen this season. It sounds a great insult, does it not? But these horse breeders take such talk for compliments. Don't let yourself be put off by it."

That Lady Jersey, top of the trees herself, was angling for an invitation to Sir Giles's estate confirmed that the gentleman was high in society. His dark eyes and smile showed his interest in Sally. He was exactly the sort of parti she had hoped to attract, and she set herself to charm him.

"You must know horses are held in the highest esteem in England, ma'am. So long as Sir Giles doesn't try to put a bit in my mouth, I have no objection to being likened to a filly." As she spoke, she swept a graceful curtsy.

"A ring on your finger is more what the gentleman has in mind, I believe."

"I really had not planned to make the offer till we had said 'How do you do,' Miss Hermitage," Sir Giles answered, "and perhaps even stood up for a dance together. I won't expect you to canter or gallop, despite my fondness for cattle."

"I am relieved to see you have no saddle in your pocket," she riposted. "But it is a set of waltzes that are coming up, and we debs, you know, are too innocent for such lively dissipation."

"Rubbish, minx," Lady Jersey decreed. "You may waltz with my blessing. There, Sir Giles, I have done all in my power to advance your case. The rest is up to you. Don't forget, now, I am on your list for Stonecroft—June the sixth, is it not?"

"I shall send you a special invitation," he promised. Then, as the music began, he took Miss Hermitage into his arms for the waltz. "I hope you are impressed with what pains I have taken to meet you," he said. "I have held Lady Jersey at bay for two seasons."

"But she is monstrously amusing!"

"Her tongue never ceases running. It's four pence to a groat she'll soon hint that the Countess Lieven would like to join us, and that is as good as saying the Prince will come along, for he is always in the Lievens' pocket."

Sally enjoyed the waltzes, but she did notice that Sir Giles held himself inordinately high. To denigrate such celebrities as the Lievens and the Prince Regent came perilously close to toploftiness. Sir Giles was attracted by her appearance, but Sally suspected that if she displayed any trace of either rusticity or fastness, she would be dropped without hesitation.

Monstuart, who had not so much as spoken to her throughout the evening, came forward as soon as Sir Giles led her from the floor. She was happy to have such an unexceptionable acquaintance to add to her consequence in front of Sir Giles. Monstuart's first utterance showed her how far this was from his intention.

His face was stiff with disapproval. "Did you not realize you're not allowed to waltz, Miss Hermitage?" he asked.

"Lady Jersey graciously gave us permission—for a price," Sir Giles said. But Monstuart's question cast a doubt on her being up to snuff. "Now that the secret is out, I suppose you are come to snatch Miss Hermitage away from me, Monty."

"My partners have been selected already, but I will be happy to try to find Miss Hermitage an escort for the next set."

"That will not be necessary, thank you, Monstuart," Sally said. Her frosty accent was all the reproof she dared risk.

"Your usual escort, Peacock, is not here, of course. They are rather careful of the clientele at Almack's."

Sir Giles looked startled; whether at the name Peacock or the rude tone of Monstuart's conversation it was difficult to tell. He looked at Sally askance.

"Mr. Peacock has no wish to attend the club," she answered hotly.

"No, indeed, it is much too respectable to suit his fancy. Gambling for chicken stakes, and not a drop of brandy or blue ruin on the premises. Why, truth to tell, Miss Hermitage, I am surprised to see *you* honor us with your presence."

"My brother-in-law, Lord Derwent, wished to come," she said, to let Sir Giles know of the connection. "And, in any case, it is an interesting contrast to Carlton House last night," she said, to inform Sir Giles of that glory.

Sir Giles did not consider Monstuart overly nice in his acquaintances, and if he was displeased with Miss Hermitage, she was obviously not his sort. He withheld the request to call on her that he had planned to make. "Thank you for the waltz, Miss Hermitage. Delightful." He bowed and left.

Sally turned a wrathful eye on Monstuart. "I hope you're satisfied!"

Monstuart lifted a black brow in simulated surprise. "Sir Giles is excellent ton. One cannot complain of his attentions. I hope he persists in them."

"A vain hope, I fear, when you were so solicitous in bringing Peacock's name forward."

"Don't raise your voice," he growled.

He grabbed her elbow and led her off to the spacious gallery of the supper room. "I hope this convinces you that Peacock is not a suitable companion for you. When his very name sends a decent man running for the hills, even you must realize what sort of creature he is."

"I can do without Sir Giles Little's notion of decency. You might be interested to know he also looks down his chiseled nose at the Prince Regent, and the Lievens and the Jerseys. Why, I come to think the man can find no companions worthy of him except Monstuart and God."

Monstuart's lips twitched in amusement. "Not necessarily in that order."

Sally noticed his softening mood. "You discouraged him on purpose. Don't bother to deny it."

"Certainly I did. The hasty wedding between Derwent and your sister showed me you played with no holds barred. I was also afraid Sir Giles meant to subject you to one of his dreadful houseparties at Stonecroft."

"They are top of the trees! I would love to have gone!"

"You only think you would have enjoyed it. His mama, a formidable Puritan dowager, is the Mistress of Ceremonies. Her idea of hellraking is a grueling session of Pope Joan, followed by an obligatory tour of the gardens, during which you admire her roses and she disparages your family connections."

"Why does everyone want to go, then?"

"Why does everyone want to attend Carlton House and Almack's? They are good ton but demmed poor entertainment."

"Whereas Mr. Peacock is bad ton but demmed good entertainment."

Monstuart's eyes narrowed, and his posture stiffened imperceptibly. "He is bad ton, in any case, and an unprincipled gambler."

"I shall be sure not to sit down to cards with him, then."

"It is clearly not money he's after in your case, nor marriage either. The man's a womanizer. Naturally you may see whom you wish, but I won't have him fleecing Derwent."

"Why tell me? I don't manage your nephew."

He gave her a blighting stare. "That is news to me." Then he hunched his shoulders and strolled away, leaving her alone.

Sally hastened back to her mother and Sir Darrow, to be handed over to another relic for the cotillion. Her evening was ruined. For a few moments, it had seemed she was getting on well with Monstuart, but they were never at peace for long. Sally wasn't sorry when they left early, but she was unhappy to hear Derwent say he was going to step down to Brook's for an hour. After the supper at the Clarendon, she spoke to Melanie.

"Why didn't you stop him? You know it is Peacock he's going to meet," Sally said after he had left. "They'll end up gambling the night away."

"How can he? He doesn't have any money" was her artless reply.

"Men gamble on credit, goose. I wish you would speak to him."

"I don't like to be pinching at him about money, when he is so very generous. Remember how Papa was always nattering to Mama, and how much she disliked it."

Sally suspected the smile her sister wore. "What extravagance has he bought you now?"

"He hasn't got it yet. Oh, Sally, it is the most romantic thing! He is buying me the Empress Josephine's sapphire-and-diamond tiara. Napoleon gave it to her when he became the emperor and then had to sell it to raise the wind for some war or other. It is going up for purchase at Sotheby's, and Ronald is getting it for me as a wedding gift. He didn't give me one, you know, except this little baguette ring of diamonds."

"You're mad! Monstuart will never allow it, and I won't allow him to squander Mama's money so foolishly."

"Oh, no! Monstuart particularly recommended it to him! He told Ronald this very evening that it is going up, and he is going to handle the transaction, so it will come out his money—the money of Ronald's that he is holding, I mean. He knows we could not possibly afford it. He asked Ronald how we are doing, and Ronald told him we have spent nearly seven thousand pounds. It is shocking how expensive everything is, and I don't really enjoy London so much, do you?"

Sally stood, with the blood draining from her cheeks. "Seven thousand! It can't be nearly that much."

"You are forgetting our presentation gowns, and stabling for all our mounts, and the opera box, and Almack's, along with the house to keep up."

"There was no need for Derwent to tell Monstuart the precise sum."

"He didn't actually tell him. They got talking about all the expenses, you know, and adding them up, and it came to seven thousand."

"You mean Monstuart weaseled it out of him, pest of a man."

"He was trying to be helpful, Sally. And then there is another thousand or so for our own ball that is coming up. I am looking forward to that. Ronald thinks Monstuart may break down and give us some of our money. He was quite pleasant tonight, don't you think?"

"I most assuredly do not."

"He was very sweet to *me*. He suggested I get a blue phaeton to match my eyes—I would be all the crack, he said. Only I don't want one. I could never drive a high-perch phaeton like Lady Dennison. She's in town, did you know? I expect that explains Monstuart's good humor."

"Very likely." Sally rose and paced the room to give vent to her temper. "I hadn't heard she is here."

"He had dinner with her, but she isn't allowed at Almack's, so he came without her."

"Naturally he couldn't miss the treat of Almack's. He doesn't even like the place."

"Ronald says that since Monty is getting us the

tiara, we must invite him to our ball. Will you invite Mr. Peacock?"

"I think not." There was no point flying in the face of polite society, and she was not so enamored of Mr. Peacock that she meant to spike her own guns.

It was a relief to hear that, despite Monstuart's continuing coolness to her, he was reaching a better footing with Ronald and Melanie. It was encroaching of him to inquire so carefully into their expenses, but there might be a good reason for it. He could hardly let them fall into debt. As Sir Darrow had said, he would look a flaming jackass if he did. That ray of hope was somewhat dimmed by Lady Dennison's arrival in town.

Chapter Eleven

Mr. Peacock came to call at Cavendish Square the next afternoon. He asked for Miss Hermitage but was equally happy to talk to Lord Derwent.

"I hoped to arrange our picnic at Richmond Park," he said.

"We'll have to speak to the ladies before setting a date," Derwent replied. "Of more interest to me, Peacock, is to have another go at faro. After picking up an easy five hundred guineas last night, I shouldn't mind having another shot. A chap can always use money."

Peacock uttered a bored laugh. "Surely money is no problem to you. You're rich as Croesus."

"My guardian holds the purse strings."

"He'd have to loosen them to pay your gambling debts. A man of honor cannot leave those hanging."

"I don't plan to lose," Derwent said. "I'm on a winning streak. I can feel it in my bones."

Peacock smiled affably. "I never saw such a natural player—and coupled with skill. If you're interested in making some real blunt, Mrs. Brody's establishment is the place. It's a private club on

Poland Street, with no limit to the stakes. She serves a tasty midnight supper. Shall we say—this evening?"

"I'm taking the ladies to a rout, but I can get away early. I'll meet you at Mrs. Brody's around eleven-thirty."

When the ladies returned, Derwent told them of Peacock's call and mentioned the picnic.

"I shall not be home whenever Mr. Peacock calls," Sally told him. "He has no reputation, Derwent. You should not see him either."

Derwent gave a superior little smile and said not a word about his plans for the late evening. When they all set out for the Eldridges' rout party, high spirits prevailed. It was enjoyable to be at last in London, attending ton parties, outfitted in fashion. The coiffeur had been called to Cavendish Square to arrange the ladies' hair. Sally had abandoned her *Grecque* style for the tousled *Victime*. It suited her well, lending a gamine touch to her appearance. She wondered whether Monstuart would comment on it, while assuring herself that she could not possibly care less what he thought.

When Monstuart proved not to be at the party, however, she was disappointed. It was a perfectly charming do. With no large balls occurring that evening, society was split up into three or four routs, with a small squeeze at each. Several of Monstuart's colleagues were at Eldridge's rout and took advantage of their leader's absence to be presented to Miss Hermitage. She had a much more interesting selection of partners than usual and was hard put to understand why the evening was so flat.

She hardly cared when Ronald suggested they

leave early. Melanie was all for it. Sir Darrow had an early case in the morning, and Mama too was agreeable to leave before midnight. As they went out to their waiting carriage, they met Monstuart just coming in. He looked surprised to see them going out the door.

"You're surely not leaving already!" he exclaimed.

Sally noticed that he directed his comment to her. She saw as well that he was not accompanied by Lady Dennison, and wondered if the affair was floundering. "Yes, we have had the carriage called," she told him.

"Where are you going? I'll say good evening to the hostess and join you soon."

"We are going home," she answered curtly. Her disappointment was rapidly turning to anger. Why must he pick this evening to be friendly, when it was impossible to take advantage of it?

"I see." He turned to Ronald to remind him of the meeting at Sotheby's at ten the next morning, said a few words to the others, and went into the rout party.

Sally was in no mood for conversation and went directly to her room when they reached Cavendish Square. She felt a peevish dissatisfaction with her Season. The men weren't so interesting as she had hoped. Peacock, who was lively, was a knave. Sir Giles Little was a boring prude, and Lord Monstuart seemed determined to annoy her.

Busy pacing her room, she didn't hear when Derwent quietly slipped down the servants' stairs and out the back door. Mellie didn't have a word of criticism to offer when her husband told her how easy it was to "pluck the Johnnie Raws" of five hundred guineas. "Don't be too late" was all she said. She even offered to tell Sally he was in bed with a headache if she asked for him.

Derwent's dissipation was not suspected by the others till he appeared at the breakfast table the next morning with red eyes and a haggard white face. Sally felt like a dishrag herself and put his appearance down to trotting too hard.

He sipped a cup of coffee while his fingertips explored the sensitive area of his temples. There seemed to be jungle drums beating inside his head. His eyes felt full of sand, and his throat was raw. He was close to nausea and, on top of that, had some dim but extremely unsettling memories of having lost rather heavily at the faro table. It was the brandy he had drunk that accounted for his state. He had never taken brandy before, but Peacock and all the chaps had been putting it back like water. Peacock would know how much he had lost. Have to speak to him this afternoon, he thought.

"Is Monstuart calling for you?" Melanie asked him. Her gentle voice sounded like thunder.

"Monty? No, why should he?"

"This is the day you're getting my tiara."

"So it is. Slipped my mind entirely. I'm meeting him there, absolutely."

"We must make arrangements for our ball this morning," Mrs. Hermitage said, and the ladies turned their thoughts to cards and flowers and refreshments. "You won't forget you are to go and see the florist this afternoon, Sal."

"I have the appointment on my schedule."

Sally's head was full of shillings and pence. She

would not order a new gown, but add rutching and pink rosebuds to her best one to give it a new look. In the midst of thoughts of shillings and rosebuds, she found herself wondering why Monstuart did not come to Cavendish Square to pick Derwent up. He had seemed friendlier last night. Perhaps he would come back afterward to see Melanie try on her tiara. So odd, to think of little Mellie wearing that dashing Empress's jewelry.

"I must be off," Derwent said soon. "Brush up your curls in readiness for the tiara, Mellie."

The morning passed quickly. Sally felt it best to set her mother to the task of writing invitations, so that she might personally oversee the ordering of supplies. She meant to keep the price as low as elegantly possible. Derwent would not want a shabby do. Even a fairly spartan ball was wickedly expensive. There must be champagne, jeroboams of it. Meats and seafoods and sweets, flowers and plants, musicians, extra help. It couldn't be done for less than a thousand pounds. She took the bad news to her mother.

"You had best sign a few checks for me, Mama, and let me fill in the sum when I get the exact figure from the merchants."

"I sign them?" her mother asked, perplexed. "Why, you must know I turned our money over to Ronald. He is the one who writes the checks for our daily expenses. It was so awkward for him having to come to me every time he wanted five or ten guineas that in the end we just sold off the Consols and put the money in Ronald's name at the bank."

Sally felt a surge of panic at this injudicious scheme. "Oh, Mama, that was foolish!"

"Don't give it a thought. Darrow worked it all up legally at five percent. I am very grateful for Darrow's help in these business matters. Never fear he would make a botch of it, for he is sharp as a needle. It is almost like having your father back, taking care of us again. And if anything should happen to Ronald, even Monstuart could not keep the money from us, for the paper is signed by Ronald and all. That is the sort of thing you or I would not have thought of, Sal. I realized the wisdom of having it in writing when Ronald looked so haggard at breakfast. A touch of flu, I expect."

"What are we to do for spending money? I am down to two guineas."

"Ask Ronald. He will be happy to give you some."

"Ronald should not have to pay our personal expenses. This becomes very complicated."

"It was easy as pie for Darrow. He is keeping track of our private spending as well. It will be deducted from Ronald's loan."

"I don't like it. Ronald is too unwise with money. I begin to regret we ever nabbed him."

"Oh, no! We would not be here, having such a good time, if we had not. I would never have met Darrow again either. . . ." She peered questioningly at her daughter. Was this the time to tell her?

Sally was already turning away. "At least we would have our fifteen thousand safe," she grumbled.

She was trying to compute how many pounds of lobster four hundred people might consume, when Ronald returned from Sotheby's. She heard the deep rumble of Monstuart's voice and hurried to the hall. The gentlemen had already entered the Saloon, and she stopped at the mirror to rearrange a wayward curl. Two flags of pink splotched her cheeks, and her eyes were sparkling. She saw Monstuart reflected in the mirror. His dark head was held at its usual proud angle. His arrogant, angular face looked handsome as he glanced around the room. Then he slowly turned toward the hall. He was looking for her! He must be; the rest of the family was already there.

When she entered the Saloon, she was careful not to look first at Monstuart, but she felt his eyes on her. When she finally condescended to greet him, he did no more than bow, but there was a conscious look in his eyes; a look of satisfaction was the closest she could come to describing it. She gave a noncommittal smile, then turned her attention to the tiara.

Ronald opened the blue velvet box, shaped like a heart and lined inside with white satin. Nestled on the satin was the beautiful jeweled piece. It rose to a high point in the center, then swept in a graceful curve to a lower crown. The pièce de résistance was a large star sapphire in the center, roughly the size of a cherry. It was encircled with diamonds. One could not but admire it, yet it seemed more suited to a queen than a modest young bride.

"I didn't think it would be so big," Melanie said. Her voice showed no admiration.

"Try it on," her husband urged. He lifted it out, put it on her head, and led her to a mirror. He tried to push it down lower on her head so that it would not rise to such startling heights.

"It looks like a crown," she objected.

Even Ronald, no connoisseur, was not entirely

happy with the effect. "You have to be dressed up to show it off," he said. "It don't look half so well with a muslin gown as it will with silk."

"I daresay it suited the Empress Josephine very well," Mrs. Hermitage said doubtfully.

"What is your opinion, Miss Hermitage?" Monstuart asked, using it as an excuse to examine her. The riot of raven curls lent her a saucy air. Her morning gown reminded him of bluebells. He longed to set the tiara on her head. She was made to wear one, as the Marchioness of Monstuart would do.

"It doesn't suit Mellie, but as a family heirloom, I suppose, it is impressive," Sally said.

"Yes, it will look well in the family collection," Mellie said, and immediately took it off.

"Dash it, Mellie, I bought it for you!" Ronald objected, becoming vexed. "Put it on and wear it."

"In the house? I am sure no one is expected to wear such a great, heavy thing around the house."

Sally glanced at the wine decanter, thinking someone ought to offer Monstuart a glass of wine, since he was being biddable in allowing Derwent to spend his money. It seemed a good opportunity to nudge him toward more practical financial leniencies.

"Would anyone care for wine?" she suggested.

Everyone accepted, and they sat down. Monstuart took a seat beside Sally on the sofa, a little removed from the others.

"Did Derwent get the tiara at a good price?" she asked.

"It was a steal at a thousand guineas."

"Were there many bidding against him?"

139

"No, we got it at the floor bid. The stones alone, if pried out, would more than return the price."

Sally frowned in perplexity. "I wonder there wasn't more competition, if that is the case."

"Only the Prince Regent was interested, and he was not in a position to offer. Odd that should have stopped him, now that I think of it," he added with a satirical grin. "Your lack of accounting skills put you in high company."

"Perhaps it is the Prince's good taste that deterred him. He has an artistic eye. If we run into shallow waters, we can always have the stones removed and sell them."

"It would be considered a savagery to dismantle the piece, with its historical associations."

Sally gave him an arch look. "I have nothing against savagery. Surely it is preferable to riding in the basket. You have unwittingly increased our money supply, Lord Monstuart."

An answering smile glowed in the depths of his deep blue eyes. "One shudders at the thought of contradicting a lady, but when the on dit is out that ladies are reduced to selling their jewels, it is as good as an announcement of bankruptcy. Nothing sends the gents running for cover more quickly."

"Your gents were running in quite a different direction last night. For some unaccountable reason, several of them were dangling after me. Odd, is it not? It never happens when you are there to keep them in line."

The look Monstuart leveled at her over his glass was not far from flirtatious. "What do you think sent me trotting to Eldridge's rout? It was the scattered nature of last night's parties that accounts for your sudden popularity. I couldn't manage all my troops. Once I determined where you were, I hastened thither to call them to account."

"Then you *are* warning them away from me!"

"Some clever person told me recently that a word to the wise is sufficient. The word gentlemen inquire for first is dowry. I felt impelled to inform them of its nonexistence. It seems my set are wise men all. Or nearly all," he added with a deliberate smile.

That smile intimated that Monstuart himself was the exception. Sally set her glass aside. The meeting was going so well that she disliked to spoil it by hinting for money. Before the words were framed, he spoke of something else.

"Some relatives of Derwent's are making a marriage visit this afternoon. Two dowager aunts—not your cup of tea, I shouldn't think."

"I have nothing against dowagers! My own mother is one."

"This pair aren't like your mama. They're coming to see how the new Lady Derwent measures up to their strict standards of propriety. You must warn her not to serve wine, and if she has a gown with long sleeves, it would not go amiss."

"I see what it is," she told him pertly. "You fear my waywardness will disgust them. I thought I showed you at Ashford that I can be second to none when I wish to behave."

"To save your from another such acting chore, I would like to take you driving with me, if you are at liberty. I am going out to a brood farm to look at a mare that is considered Derby material. Will you come?"

Sally was doubly distressed to have to miss such a pleasant diversion and to refuse Monstuart's offer. It was not imagination, then, that he had been friendlier last night. "Unfortunately, I am busy this afternoon."

His eyebrow quirked up with interest. "My ruse with Sir Giles was unsuccessful, was it?"

"No, Lord Monstuart. He frightens too easily. You succeeded in alienating him, with your solicitous mention of Peacock."

The eyebrow rose higher, and his smile stiffened. "Is it Peacock you're seeing this afternoon?"

"No, it is the florist," she said petulantly. "A ball does not arrange itself, you know."

His eyebrow fell immediately, and his smile thawed. "I am happy to hear you're not seeing Peacock. Some very unsavory stories are beginning to surface regarding him. It seems his pockets aren't so deep as he let on. What money he has he gets from sheering the young. He plays with them at some decent place the first night and lets them win a little something. They're led to Mrs. Brody's gaming parlor for the kill. He has an interest in a gaming establishment fronted by a Mrs. Brody. I fancy that's his own name. He has an Irish charm about him."

"Which is more than can be said for Sir Giles. He has a very English sangfroid."

"As to Sir Giles, if he is so easily frightened, he's not the man for you. What have you all got planned for this evening?"

Sally peered at him from the corner of her eyes. "Why, milord, Lady Dennison will be angry with

142

you, neglecting her so shamelessly after bringing her to town."

"I did not *bring* her to town! She comes every Season. We are friends, no more."

The alacrity and vehemence of his rejoinder pleased her. It was beginning to seem that Monstuart was freeing himself of all encumbrances. One could not but wonder at it, even hope.

"We are attending the play at Drury Lane," she replied.

"I think you will enjoy it. Kean did a fine job as Lear. I shan't be attending, but you must by all means make use of that season's ticket. Where will you go afterward?"

"We have cards for Engleworth's ball."

"Excellent. So have I."

Miss Hermitage was in very good spirits when Monstuart took his leave. It wasn't till Ronald took up the tiara to examine it that she fell into a pelter.

"It's a pity I bought this thing, since you don't care for it," he said to Melanie. His mouth looked sulky. "A waste of blunt, and we haven't any to spare."

"Monstuart paid for it out of your own money, did he not?" Sally asked.

"No, I thought he meant to, but when it was time to pay up, he asked me if I had brought cash or meant to write a check. Said it right in front of the fellow at Sotheby's, you know, so there was nothing for it but to give them a check. I daresay he thought I didn't have the blunt, but *I* showed him."

"You spent our money on this ugly thing!" she charged.

"I'm paying interest," he retorted.

The blood rushed to Sally's head, and her lungs felt suffocated. "He did it on purpose! The wretched sneak! He is trying to bankrupt us, so we will have to rusticate at Gravenhurst. That's why he was in such a chirping mood, because he thought he had outwitted us. And he has. Oh, Ronald, I wish you had not bought it when you learned the truth. Why did you not refuse?"

"Wouldn't satisfy him. Besides, everybody at Sotheby's congratulated me. It's a bargain," he insisted, frowning at the gaudy ornament. "The only pity is that it looks so awful on Mellie."

Mellie looked hard at him but decided the slur was on the bibelot, not her.

"Where does this leave us?" Sally said, speaking aloud but really talking to herself, for the others were obviously no accountants.

She got out a piece of paper and pen and began toting up figures. So many thousands had already miraculously melted away, a thousand for the ball, a thousand for that ugly crown. Derwent went and hung over her shoulder.

"Seven thousand left, and we have already spent eight in one month," she sighed.

"Actually, six thousand left," Derwent said. "There were a few incidentals—my dues at Tatt's and Brook's, you know."

"It's a pity you joined Brook's. Don't play too deep, Derwent, but at least it's better than getting fleeced by the Captain Sharps. I ought to warn you away from that Peacock fellow. It's a good thing we dropped him. Monstuart says he is a regular crook. Between shaved cards and loaded dice, I daresay he

144

never loses. If he ever invites you to Mrs. Brody's parlor, be sure you refuse."

Derwent gulped, and his eyes stared. "Eh?"

"That is where he fleeces the flats. He lets them win a couple of hundred first, then the next night he takes them to Brody's and picks them clean. Oh, and there is your annual allowance," Sally continued. "We left that out." With her eyes on her figures, she failed to notice Derwent's reaction. "We must retrench severely," she continued, all unaware of Derwent's turmoil.

How much had he lost last night? He had to see Peacock at once. Dashed crook. He wouldn't pay him a sou. Why should he? He had even felt the shaved edge of the cards but thought it must be the brandy making them fuzzy.

Across the room, Mrs. Hermitage said to her younger daughter, "Ronald looks a little peaky. I can't think why, when we had such an early night."

Melanie looked at the tiara and thought that explained her husband's mood. "I won't have to wear it at my ball, will I?" she asked.

"No, dear. We'll just have Ronald put it in the vault with all the other great, unwearable lumps. Pity it hadn't been a string of pearls or a small set of diamonds, but he meant well. What time are Ronald's relatives coming?"

"At four."

It was not necessary for Derwent to go looking for Peacock. He received a note, with a mention of five thousand in I.O.U.s, asking when Derwent would like to settle and suggesting a meeting that evening at midnight. There was an air of menace about the curt note. Peacock requested cash, not a check, and said he "was in urgent need of payment." Peacock had seemed on very close terms with the rough-looking set at Brody's Parlor. What would they do if he reneged? Someone had mentioned Peacock's skill with dueling pistols.

A man with a brand-new bride couldn't put himself in such jeopardy. He'd just have to pay up. Own up, pay up, shut up—it was the gentleman's creed. Derwent was more than willing to comply with the last item. Naturally he wouldn't say a word to the ladies. He looked again at the note. Mr. Peacock would be happy to call at Cavendish Square, a contingency to be avoided at all costs. His servant, a bruiser with a broken nose and an arm like a leg, waited for a reply.

With trembling hand, Lord Derwent wrote his reply, suggesting midnight outside of Brook's. He had just time to nip down to the bank and get the five thousand in cash before lunch. How his new family was to hobble along on one thousand pounds was a matter to be worked out. With luck, his aunts might bring along a little something as a wedding gift.

Chapter Twelve

As Sally dressed for the evening, half her pleasure was stolen by worries. The stunning white silk
gown had cost too much, though it rustled beautifully when she walked and the twinkling of sequins
through the chiffon overskirt gave exactly the effect she had hoped for, like stars peering from behind clouds. She pondered how she should repay
Monstuart for his latest vile deception, for it went
without saying that he must be repaid. He was ex-
acting a hard revenge for her success in getting
Derwent to marry Melanie. It was perfectly obvious
his scheme was to get them all out of town as soon
as possible, and at the rate they were spending, that
would be within the week.

The best revenge would be to stay the Season and
nab a prize parti herself. But with Monstuart whispering in all their ears that she was a solicitor's
dowerless daughter, how was she to accomplish it?
What irked most of all was his duplicity in coming
that same morning to flirt with her. How would he
behave this evening, at Engleworth's ball? Would
he continue the charade of friendship, stand up with

her, flirt? Was he foolish enough to think she didn't see what he was up to?

If so, she'd put his apparent approval to good use and get introductions to as many of his friends as possible. Surely one of them would prove susceptible to black curls and green eyes. Her body occupied a seat at the theater for the first part of the evening, but her mind was already at the ball.

Sally was not the only member of the party whose mind was not on Kean's performance. Derwent sat like a martyr, silent, morose, as he pondered his own problem. He hadn't really expected much from his aunts Theodora and Rosalie. They meant well by giving him and Mellie the rose tea set, very likely, and at least Mellie liked it, but cash would have been more welcome. From time to time he patted the bulge of five thousand pounds in his inner pocket.

The thing to do was escort the ladies to the ball after the play, have a dance with Mellie, then nip quickly over to Brook's and give Peacock the money. He'd be back within two shakes of the lamb's tail, and no one would be any the wiser. This venture into the world of gambling and vice had taught him his lesson. From now on he'd walk the straight and narrow, but by Jove it was hard to do with the temptations of London. Should have gone to Gravenhurst as he wanted to in the first place. Mellie wouldn't mind a bit. Of course, there was Sally to be considered.

Mrs. Hermitage had her problem, too, though it was such a pleasant problem that she could hardly keep from smiling, all through the tragedy of King Lear. Sir Darrow had asked her to marry him. Of course, she had accepted. The only question, really, was when to do it. Darrow said they had wasted enough time, and he wanted to marry her immediately. She thought it better to wait till the Season was over. A wedding to arrange on top of their ball was almost more excitement than she could envisage. Then, too, it would mean Sal had to leave Derwent's house and come with her and Darrow, and she knew Sal had her heart set on making her bows from the home of a lord. One did not voluntarily put Sal in one of her pelters.

Only Melanie sat contentedly. She had no problem. She was married to the most handsome, generous man in London. As soon as the Season was over, she would be able to escape all the bustle of London and go with him to Gravenhurst and live happily ever after. Her fairytale had come true. Except that if Sally didn't find a husband of her own, she might come to Gravenhurst with them. While Melanie loved her sister dearly, she admitted there were times when she would much rather be alone with Derwent. Her mind roamed over possible partis. Monstuart seemed to have some tendre for Sal. Perhaps she could help advance a match in that quarter.

When the group stood at the top of Lady Engleworth's staircase, having their names announced, Sally peered to the crowd below. Her eyes narrowed when she saw Monstuart fast advancing to greet them. His eager expression might easily be mistaken for approval, but he had deceived her for the last time. She would be as sweet as honey, she would wrest any good his apparent approval could give her, but she would show this man a lesson yet.

Monstuart greeted the group but soon turned his attention to Sally. "How did you enjoy the play?" he asked.

She gave him a flirtatious glance and replied, "My heart was not in the mood for tragedy. I kept thinking of this lovely ball I was missing, and my only mood was impatience."

"Then we shared an emotion, even if we were not together."

This came dangerously close to sentiment. She knew Monstuart was about as sentimental as a dagger, and decided to goad him to further excesses of folly. "How could you be impatient for the ball? You were already here, Lord Monstuart."

"But *you* weren't." He tucked her hand under his arm and led her off. "It was you I was waiting for. Now you have heard what you wished to. I promise I shan't bethump with you any more maudlin compliments. Shall we dance?"

Sets were forming for a cotillion. "Let us wait for a waltz," she suggested. "It is so much more ... personal, and once we have stood up together, we have nothing further to look forward to for the evening."

"I think we might have two dances together without raising any eyebrows."

She gave him a flirtatious smile. "You think wrong, Lord Monstuart. Every quiz in the room would whisper that you were showing a great deal of attention to Miss Hermitage."

His dark gaze lingered on her, and his lips lifted a fraction in an incipient smile. "Worse, they would say you had caught me."

She decided to take offense. "You aren't the one

who will look a fool when it all comes to nothing. We ladies have our pride to consider, you know."

Monstuart gazed at her long-lashed eyes and the beautiful contrast of ebony hair against that ivory skin. His reply was delayed a moment. "You have decided it will come to nothing, have you?"

She peered coquettishly from the corner of her eyes. Her heart pounded in excitement and anger. "You must know a lady never reveals her feelings till she is certain they are reciprocated. Now that I am in London, I must leave off country manners."

Monstuart inclined his head close to hers. His voice was softly intimate. "I think I preferred us in Ashford. Will it offend you if I choose your next partner?"

She followed the line of his eyes to see a middle-aged gentleman looking in their direction. "It will if old Gouty Sudderland is the gent you have in mind."

"I don't want to give myself too much competition."

Her lashes flickered shamelessly. "You are too modest, Monstuart. You know there isn't a gentleman in the room who provides real competition for you."

A bark of laughter cracked out. "This sentiment is contagious. We must take care, or we'll be out picking flowers in sun-dappled pastures. Very well, tell me who it is you have in your eye."

She chose Lord Alton, one of Monstuart's set, a handsome, wealthy nobleman. "You realize there is a price for the introduction," he warned.

"I have already promised you the first set of waltzes, Lord Monstuart."

"That has already been established. The bonus I refer to is that you stop calling me Lord Monstuart as though we were mere acquaintances. My friends call me Monty."

"Very well, Monty."

"And I shall ask your sister to stand up with me. She no longer hates me, I think. I have been at some pains to bring her around. You are observing, I trust, how far my guileless mind is from providing *you* any competition."

"This seems an auspicious moment for you to assure me I am above competition."

"Since you already know it, you save me the trouble."

Lord Alton proved a charming partner. Sally was sure that if her mind had been on romance, she might have made some headway with him, for he was admiring. Her second partner, another of Monstuart's friends, was equally suitable. But her mind was not on romance. Anger seethed in her breast at Monstuart's duplicity. How he must be anticipating her disgrace! Why was he pretending to like her? The answer came slowly, but at length she had figured it out. He was only making up to her to ensure that she didn't form any other attachment! It was exactly the sort of underhanded stunt she expected from him. When bellowing her lack of dowry didn't turn the trick, he pretended he loved her.

With so much on her mind, Sally didn't notice that Derwent was missing for a set. Mrs. Hermitage, occupied with Sir Darrow in the card parlor, didn't notice it either. Derwent told his bride he was stepping out to blow a cloud but would be back presently. She was not such a sleuth that she noticed the lack of tobacco reek when he returned from his rendezvous with Peacock half an hour later.

When the set of waltzes began, Monstuart appeared at Sally's elbow. "At last," he said, and drew her into his arms. His words called to mind Peacock, who had said the same thing. It seemed her fate to be surrounded by faithless scoundrels.

They floated around the room as lightly as feathers. Monstuart thought the febrile glitter in her eyes and her air of breathless excitement was due to pleasure. He felt unusually animated himself. The step he was anticipating was one he had avoided for years. Marriage was a large, irrevocable step, but one he must take eventually.

Sally Hermitage made the step not only possible but enjoyable. She was a woman whose charms would not pall after the first month. A gentleman must marry an innocent bride, but that was no reason she must be a Bath Miss. Sally was conversable, she was intelligent, and she was beautiful. In short, she represented the best of all possible brides: virtue robed in the alluring guise of a mistress.

He was done fighting the inevitable. She had bested him in rushing Derwent's marriage forward. He had made some rallying and halfhearted efforts at repaying her, but the thing was done. It would be petty and fruitless to fight it further. Sally would have no trouble finding a husband, and to risk losing her was unthinkable. He must give Derwent at least some of his money. But they would speak of that later. For now he would let his body and head reel through this delicious waltz.

When it was over, he said, "If we go to the refreshment parlor, we can prolong this meeting."

"And you can avoid the strenuous exertion of the country dance," she riposted. "I have noticed you always avoid them, Monty. Don't bother letting on that staying in my company has anything to do with it."

He smiled, unfazed at her charge of selfishness. "Wouldn't you like to hear the cool trickle of the punch fountain?" he tempted.

"Not in the least, but I wouldn't mind slaking my thirst on a glass of champagne."

They sat in a private corner, half-hidden by a spreading palm, and talked the greatest nonsense. "Is London living up to your expectations?" Monstuart asked.

"Now that you have permitted the eligible bachelors to recognize me, it surpasses them."

"Would it assuage your vanity if I admitted what a hard time I have had holding them back?"

"You surely don't expect to trap me into admitting vanity by that loaded question?"

"Vanity was the wrong word. I should have said pride. That is a good Anglo-Saxon virtue. I am virtuous myself, in that one respect."

"And no other?" she asked, batting her eyes in mock horror.

"I lay claim to all the gentleman's virtues. I never seduce innocent ladies or fail to pay my gambling debts or vote Conservative," he joked.

Sally observed the cynical nature of his answer but failed to notice his joking mood. "Papa always voted Conservative."

"He got a deal of business from them."

She felt the prickle of anger that could no longer be controlled. "And what do you get from the Whigs, Monstuart?"

"Peace of conscience. I don't parade my philanthropy, but any man with a heart has to support the reforms of the Whigs. Have I surprised you? You thought because you only see me in society that I have no other interests? What you imagined to be an orgy at Lady Dennison's was, in fact, a meeting of Whigs planning to wrest power and reform the electoral ridings. We deem it unfair that Lord Suddaby's barn has a vote in parliament, whereas many towns of ten or twelve thousand have not."

It was the first time she had heard Monstuart speak of such serious things, and she looked alarmed. That he should come out on the side of the underprivileged was as surprising as the rest.

"I hope I have impressed you," he admitted. "I wouldn't want you to think I was only a fashionable fribble or that my wife would have no more strenuous duties than being popular."

Wife! She was ambushed by the word and all it implied. An air of constraint came over her. She looked uncertainly at him and felt terribly ill at ease.

"I've chosen a poor moment to speak of politics," he said at once. "Blame it on my lust for your approval. And now, if you've had all the champagne you can hold, I'll take you back to the ballroom. You haven't stood up with Derwent yet," he said laughing. "Fair is fair. I hauled Mellie around the floor. You must submit to Derwent's two left feet."

Derwent was found and agreed sulkily to stand up with Sally. "I have a ripping headache, if you want the truth," he complained. "Mellie don't like London above half, and I come to think I don't either." Gravenhurst would be a much cheaper place to rusticate. The difficulty was Mrs. Hermitage and Sally.

"The Season only lasts six weeks. There is plenty of time for Gravenhurst."

"The Season is more than half over. I don't see why we can't leave at once."

"And cheat Melanie of her ball? Derwent, don't be so selfish. It is all arranged."

"The cards ain't out yet." And more important, none of the expensive orders had arrived. No reason it couldn't all be canceled and save a thousand pounds. "It's dashed expensive, entertaining half of London."

"Half of London has entertained us. Social obligations must be repaid."

"Oh, absolutely."

"And what of the expensive house in Cavendish Square?"

"I know a chap who'd sublet and pay nearly the whole price we paid for the entire Season, for as time goes on, places are impossible to hire."

Sally fell into alarm to learn he was actively working to leave London. "Don't be ridiculous!" she scoffed. "We're not that poor. We still have six thousand pounds—haven't we?"

Derwent scowled and stumbled on to the next step of the dance. You could have bowled him over with a zephyr when Tinny Hendry was standing there with Peacock, also with his fist full of I.O.U.s. Another thousand pounds. It came as close to wiping him out as made no difference. And how was he to tell the ladies? Lord Derwent felt like Atlas, trying to plod up a hill with a great weight on his back.

If it were only he and Mellie, there would be nothing to it. It seemed hard that a man had to deal with his bride's whole family, and Monstuart thrown into the bargain, making him buy that ugly tiara that Mellie hated. Maybe he could sell it. When the steps of the dance brought Sally back to him, she repeated, "Haven't we got six thousand left, Derwent?"

"Of course we have." He scowled. There was something in her green stare that unmanned him.

As soon as the dance was over, Derwent took Melanie home. "You tell Mama we decided to leave," Melanie said to her sister.

Sally was concerned and spoke to her mother as soon as she left the card table. Her mother brushed it aside. "It is only natural they should want their house to themselves from time to time," she said archly. "Newlyweds—and to have the pair of us forever hanging over their shoulders like vultures."

"They have plenty of time to themselves. The house is huge. They need only see us at meals if they want to."

Mrs. Hermitage sighed. "It's different when you're in love, Sal. You never were sensitive to the finer emotions."

"I don't like it," Sally insisted. "He even spoke of returning to Gravenhurst—immediately, before the ball. What has he got in his head?"

Mrs. Hermitage looked interested at this news. If Derwent took Mellie off to Gravenhurst, there would be nothing to delay her own match with Darrow. Sally would no longer have the prestige of being under Lord Derwent's roof, so she couldn't object to removing to Darrow's apartment. Except that it really was too small for the three of them.

"You don't mean it," she said pensively. "What would he do with Cavendish Square?"

"He mentioned subletting it. Did you ever hear of anything so foolish?"

"Subletting, you say?" It flashed into her mind in an instant that Darrow could sublet, and they wouldn't even have the bother of moving. He could just move in with them till the lease was up.

"More to the point, what are *we* to do? We'll have to go home. It will be pretty tight, living in Ashford when we've spent so much of our money."

"Ashford? I don't intend to return there, Sal. It is like a stagnant pond, after the pleasure of London."

London had given Sally about as much pleasure as a bad tooth. "Perhaps one of us will have Heppleworth after all," she said wearily.

"Surely not! You can do better than that, Sal."

"Actually, Mama, it was you I had in mind. I only said it to frighten you into talking some sense into Mellie, in the hope that she will persuade Derwent out of this freakish idea."

Mrs. Hermitage patted her curls and said, "Darrow might have something to say to my marrying Heppleworth."

It took a moment for her meaning to sink in. "You don't mean he has offered!"

"Several times, and I haven't said no."

"Oh, Mama! How lovely for you."

"For us all, Sal. We will want you to live with us. We'll have a good cose when we get home." Then she strode out of the room, leaving Sally behind with a musing smile on her face. Mama and Sir Darrow—what a boon that would be! It seemed all the family was having success except her. It never occurred to her that her mother would marry immediately, which still left her with the problem of Derwent's wanting to leave London.

Monstuart rushed forward as soon as he saw Sally alone. "I hadn't the foresight to ask you to join me for supper," he said. "I hope I am not too late."

"I'm promised to Sir Darrow Willowby's table, Monstuart."

His black brow rose quizzically. "Monstuart? We leaped that hurdle when last I spoke to you. I was hoping to be calling you Sally before the evening is over."

He frowned at her lack of attention. She didn't invite him to use her name, or forbid it, or utter any of the light sort of banter he had been expecting. "Is something the matter, Miss Hermitage?" he asked.

"Derwent and Mellie have gone home," she said.

"That is hardly a tragedy. They are newlyweds, after all."

"Yes, it seems to be contagious."

His black brow rose imperceptibly. He had not said anything definite enough to warrant that assumption. "Like the plague," he agreed blandly.

"I must join Sir Darrow now. Good evening, Monstu—Monty."

"Must I say good evening, Miss Hermitage?"

"No, you may say '*au revoir*.' I trust we shall be meeting again soon."

"Very soon. *Au revoir*, Mam'selle."

Sally darted to Sir Darrow to congratulate him. Her face was wreathed in smiles. "Are congratulations premature, Papa?" she asked pertly.

"Ho, sly minx. You have weaseled it out of Mabel, I see. Well, it is true. She has been foolish enough to have me. I can manage her, but what I am to do with you I have no idea. I'm too old to be turning the bucks off the premises. You must hop to it and find yourself a husband."

She wagged his chin playfully. "All the best ones are taken." She smiled.

He grabbed her hand and kissed it. "On the other hand, I shouldn't mind having such a bright pair of eyes in the house for a few months."

Monstuart watched the meeting with rising consternation. He hadn't observed this playfulness between Sally and Willowby before. And the mother looking on as placid as may be. Was it possible she was promoting a match between that old slice and Sal? She had certainly encouraged the walking pharmacopeia in Ashford. He felt a shudder of revulsion but no fear that Willowby provided him any real competition. All the same, he would make his offer very soon. His friends were finding Sally too attractive for his peace of mind.

At Cavendish Square, Lord Derwent quickly drank up half a bottle of wine and confessed his sins to Lady Derwent. Her reaction couldn't have been more understanding if he'd written the script himself.

"I never liked Peacock above half," she told him. "What a wretched person he is, just the kind of man Sally *would* introduce to you."

"By Jove, I never would have met him on my

own, for he isn't let into any decent club. How was a gentleman supposed to know how the likes of him carried on?"

"You're too good to even think of anyone cheating at cards," she assured him. "I fear London is a wicked place, Ronald. We were happier in Ashford, were we not? With those nice drives and walks in the countryside and family dinner parties. We never get to sit together in London, and at the balls, we have to dance with other people. I even had to stand up with Monstuart."

Derwent was completely sympathetic to this fate. "We could be together more at Gravenhurst," he pointed out, "and it wouldn't cost us a sou."

"But we'd have Sally with us," she reminded him. This certainly took the bloom off the idyll. "Unless Monstuart agreed to repay Mama's money, and they could go back to Ashford," she added diffidently. She knew Ronald disliked speaking to Monty about money. "We can hardly ask Sally to speak to Monstuart," she pointed out. "Not when she will have her jaw set against the plan."

"It would almost be worth risking speaking to him myself," he said uncertainly. "Sal will be in a rare pelter at Gravenhurst with the ball cancelled and having to cut short the Season before she nabs a husband."

"Why don't you write to Monty?" Melanie suggested. "That way he won't be able to say anything nasty."

"Clever minx, that's the ticket. And you must help me butter him up. It ain't as if we're asking for the moon, after all. It's my money."

"I shall tell Mama," Mellie said bravely. "She

never cuts up stiff. She knows how easy it is to spend money, so she'll understand."

"You're the best, bravest wife in the world, Mellie. I don't deserve you."

Lady Derwent smiled contentedly. "Yes, you do," she said generously. They debated the point for as long as possible to stave off writing to Monstuart, but at last Derwent had his way. He was unworthy of her, and to achieve worthiness he bravely took up pen and wrote to his guardian, explaining in confusing detail that he needed some of his own money for a pressing matter, if it would not be too inconvenient.

"You write beautifully," Melanie said. "Let us not send the letter till tomorrow, or Monstuart will come charging in at breakfast and spoil the whole day. If you send it around eleven, he won't come till three or four."

"And that will give you time to speak to your mama in the morning."

They exchanged a loving look of complete understanding and went upstairs to take advantage of their solitude.

Chapter Thirteen

Lady Derwent found it easier to confess Ronald's sins to her mother than to Sally. Mrs. Hermitage, with her own profitable union to buttress her against poverty, proved not at all condemning when Melanie cornered her in the privacy of her bedroom the next morning for the revelation.

"It is shocking the way money evaporates in London. There was never anything like it," she said, shaking her head in mystery. "So that is why you are going to Gravenhurst. I found it excessively odd when Sally mentioned it last evening. When are you planning to leave?"

"Right away, Mama."

"Immediately? Oh, dear, will you not be here for the wedding, then?"

"Wedding! You never mean Sally has had an offer! Who was it from?"

"Sally? No such a thing. Who would ever offer for—not to say she is unattractive, but such a tongue! She turns all the fellows off with it. Darrow is marrying me."

Melanie was delighted with the news. "When?

she asked after a few repetitions of all the customary compliments.

"As soon as possible. I have been trying to put him off till the Season is over, for I was afraid Sal would cut up stiff if she had to leave Cavendish Square. But if you and Ronald are leaving in any case, it begins to look as if we must speed up the marriage. We can do it by special license. Then Darrow can sublet this place from Ronald, and we shall all go on living here—Sally and Darrow and I, I mean. The rent from this place will give Ronald a little money to get you two to Gravenhurst."

After going over the logistics a few times, the advantages of the scheme were finally clear to Melanie, and she sent off for Ronald to join them. He entered the room diffidently, casting a frightened face at his wife. Mellie was smiling so sweetly that he knew she had smoothed his path.

"That's something like," he said, beaming, when he was let in on the secret. "I'm sorry I bothered to dash that note off to Monstuart. We might have kept the whole thing from him, for your mother won't need her blunt right away, now that she is marrying Willowby."

"There is still Sally to consider," Mrs. Hermitage pointed out. "She would have something to say about your nipping off and leaving her without a sou. For that matter, I would be happy to have the money back myself. Weddings are very dear, and I dislike to dun Darrow for money before we are shackled."

"Sally will be in the boughs," Melanie agreed. "Especially when she learns we are canceling our ball. She quite looked forward to it."

"Canceling the ball?" Mrs. Hermitage asked in alarm. "Oh, my dear, who will tell her that?"

The two pairs of pleading eyes directed at her gave her a hint as to who was to do the deed. She began fanning herself vigorously. "One thing at a time," she decided. "She was chirping merry at my engagement to Darrow last night. After she has got over her fit when she learns you two are leaving, I shall talk up the advantages of my match, and when she is in a good mood sometime, I'll tell her."

"But it must be soon, Mama," Mellie urged, "or she will go ahead and mail the invitations."

Fate cast a few rubs in the path of the conspirators. The first was that Lord Monstuart was not at home when Derwent's note was delivered. He had made a dashing visit to his own country estate in Berkshire and was not expected back for two days. That same morning a letter arrived from the estate agent in Ashford who had been trying to sublet the Hermitages' house there. He had found a taker who wanted immediate occupancy, which meant someone had to go to Ashford to tie up the details and attend to the packing.

It struck all three conspirators that getting Sally out of the house on Cavendish Square for a few days would be an advantage. As they fully expected, however, she scotched their plan.

"I cannot sign the lease over, Mama. It is in your name. In any case, I shall be fully occupied here, arranging the ball." Sally had taken control of plans for this grand occasion, and no one had yet found the courage to tell her she worked in vain.

"I have some planning to do myself," Mrs. Hermitage said with an air of importance. Sally looked

165

at her expectantly. "I told you—I am marrying Darrow."

"You don't have to begin plans so soon, surely."

"We have decided not to wait, Sal. We are going to get a special license and get married right away."

"What is the rush?"

"You know Ronald and Mellie want to leave London. Unless we wish to go to Gravenhurst with them, I must marry now, or you and I will have nowhere to lay our heads."

"There's no reason *we* must go. This house is hired for the Season."

"They plan to sublet," Mrs. Hermitage said, not without a quiver of apprehension.

Sally's eyes darkened. "The cheek of that Derwent! He spends our money, then plans to hire the house out from under us. Well, we'll take the sublet money and hire something smaller."

"Oh, my dear, would it not be nicer to stay on here?"

Sally blinked in confusion. "Indeed it would, but you said he means to sublet."

"To Darrow! That is, I have not told him yet, but he will be needing a larger place for the three of us."

The advantages of this scheme were not long in occurring to Sally. "Yes, I see. If you and Sir Darrow think it will do, I have nothing to say against it. But you still must go and tend to business in Ashford, Mama. It will only take a few days. Sir Darrow can get the license while you are away, and I shall arrange a small wedding party here. Will that not accomplish all the necessities with the minimum of time and bother?"

Driving all the way to Ashford seemed like a very large minimum to Mrs. Hermitage, but she knew her wayward daughter would have her way in the end, and gave up arguing. Sir Darrow was consulted and agreed with this plan. Derwent and Melanie, who awaited Monstuart's return, were consigned to remaining in London. As the wedding was to occur in four days' time, they would stay for that as well, whether Monstuart gave them their money or not. And through it all, it was kept from Sally that Derwent had lost all their money and the much anticipated ball would not take place.

Before Mrs. Hermitage left for Ashford the next morning, she ordered Sir Darrow to keep Sally fully occupied with wedding plans, to prevent her from ordering anything else for the ball. He took his duty seriously and spent every possible moment in her company.

She did not accompany him to the Bishop for the license, but she was deeply involved in everything else. "We shall have the little dinner party at Clarendon's Hotel," he decided. "It will save you the fuss of arranging one at home."

She accompanied him to Clarendon's to order dinner and wine. "A *potage de poissons à la Russe* to begin," Sir Darrow said. Despite his small size, he was an excellent trencherman. "Followed by *l'oie braisée aux champignons*, or would some *filets de volaille* sit better? A side dish of *épinards à l'essence*—we must have our greens. A saddle of mutton—we want some good English bulk in our diet."

"We also want to be able to get into our gowns!"

"You could all put on another stone and still be sylphs. We'll fill you up on entremets. Let me see, now—*les genoises glacées au caramel*, with perhaps a plate of *petites souffles d'abricots*, to eke out the chantilly and cream buns. That will do for starters. Let us see the wine list, lad. Champagne, mind! I won't get married to the tune of claret."

After the menu was settled, Sir Darrow went to the theater and arranged a private performance at the house on Cavendish Square for after the wedding dinner. Some actors and musicians who were "at leisure" were happy to oblige him. He wished to invite a few dozen of his best friends for this concert and urged Sally to do likewise. "Is there anyone in particular you would like to ask?"

Sally was curious that Monstuart had not called and said, "Perhaps we should invite Lord Monstuart."

"He is out of town."

"I hadn't heard!"

Nor would Sir Darrow have heard if Mrs. Hermitage had not told him. "That is what they are saying in the clubs. Anyone else?"

She mentioned a few friends. That afternoon she wrote invitations and delivered them with Sir Darrow.

That evening she accompanied him to the opera, along with Derwent and Melanie. The next morning he called again, determined to keep her busy.

"We shall take a run downtown and pick out your mama's wedding ring this morning," he told her.

"Delightful!"

"And a little wedding gift of some sort. Diamonds, I expect. I notice she never wears the set the Hermit gave her. Pawned them, I suppose?"

"Eons ago, Sir Darrow. I believe they paid for our remove from Bath to Ashford."

He shook his head fondly. "Shatter-brained girl."

The gaudy set of diamonds he chose for the wedding gift told Sally that money was no object to Sir Darrow. He wanted to pick up a trifling diamond bracelet for her as well, but she firmly forbade it.

"I cannot order you about yet, Missie, but after the wedding, we shall see who has his way." He smiled fondly. "By the living jingo, we have forgotten the most important thing! The wedding ring. Pick out a nice one."

A few other customers looked at the unlikely couple and shook their heads. Among them was Monstuart's friend Lord Alton. He remained in the background but kept his ears cocked.

Sally looked over the tray of rings. Aware that Sir Darrow's choice was for large gems, she suggested an emerald-cut diamond of ten carats.

"Put it on your finger. Let us see how it looks 'on,' as you ladies say."

She slid the ring on her finger and held it out. Blue and orange and green fire danced in its depths. "It's beautiful, Sir Darrow."

"Keep it on your finger. It's the safest place for it. Sure I can't tempt you with a bracelet?"

"Hold on to your blunt. You will find us an expensive tribe."

"Ho, ho. I can't say I wasn't warned. Mabel said the same thing, but you are worth every penny of it. Money was made to be spent."

Sir Darrow and Miss Hermitage became a familiar sight in London. Tongues were soon wagging. It was inevitable that when Lord Monstuart returned, he heard whispers of what was going forth. Even before he entered his own mansion, he was stopped by a friend of Alton's.

"You have led us all up the garden path, Monty," his friend joked. "We thought you were saving Miss Hermitage for yourself. If I'd known she'd marry just anyone, I would have offered for her."

Monstuart's black eyebrow rose to an alarming height. "Miss Hermitage is engaged? May I know who the man is?"

"Old Willowby, a friend of her papa."

"Sir Darrow Willowby?"

"That's the gent. He's well to grass, of course, but really! An ankle-biter—he doesn't come past her shoulder, and he must be all of sixty. They look like an Amazon and Father Time on the strut together. She hangs on his arm, delighted with her catch."

"You're mistaken," Monstuart said coldly. "He's Mrs. Hermitage's beau."

"Devil a bit of it. The mother was only a cover-up. They've dispensed with her now. Alton saw the pair of them picking out the ring. A very large one, *ça va sans dire*. A case of cream-pot love, obviously. Their major outings are to the shops."

Monstuart's nostrils quivered in distaste. "Very interesting," he said in the most bored tone he could muster.

His instinct was to pelt directly to Cavendish Square, but discretion urged him to get his temper under control first. He went home and was given Lord Derwent's letter. After much discussion with his wife, Derwent had written, "Dear Monstuart: Due to circumstances beyond my control, I find I have need of fifteen thousand pounds of my own money. Lady Derwent and I wish to go to Gravenhurst, for London is very dear. As the fifteen thousand is owed to Lady Derwent's mother, I am sure you will see that I must have it immediately. I won't ask for any more except my allowance until I reach my maturity. Sincerely, your nephew, Derwent."

Monstuart's jaws clenched in disgust. He squashed the note into a ball and threw it into the grate. He soon retrieved it and read it again, looking for the fine hand of Miss Hermitage between the lines. It was lurking there, in every word. The ladies had lent Derwent their money, spent it, and were now demanding it back. They had lured Derwent into their velvet trap while his own back was turned. Derwent was Miss Hermitage's ticket to London. Dissatisfied with the aging Heppleworth's provincial charms, she had schemed her way to London to nab a larger fortune.

Now that Derwent had served his purpose, he was being dispatched home, but if she thought to recover her mother's money into the bargain, she was mistaken. Not one sou would he give Derwent. Mrs. Hermitage must make her abode with either Derwent or the Willowbys. These cogitations did not have the desired effect of diluting Monstuart's temper. Quite the contrary, the longer he thought, the higher his anger mounted. When he called for his curricle and leaped into the driver's seat, his face was an alarming hue.

It did not lighten when he saw Sir Darrow coming jauntily out of the door of the house on Cavendish Square, and Sally there, waving him good-bye.

"Monstuart, so you are back!" Sir Darrow smiled.

"Miss Hermitage will be happy to see you. She was hoping to invite you to the wedding."

"Go to hell," Monstuart growled, and bounded up the stairs two at a time. Sir Darrow shook his head in confusion and went on his way. Queer nabs, young Monstuart, but he need not fear he would frighten Sal. She had the heart of a lion, like her papa.

Sally's heart pounded when she saw her caller's foul mood. She felt a strong desire to slam the door and bolt it, but before she could accomplish this, Monstuart was in, towering above her like Wrath incarnate. His forbidding aspect set her hackles up. "I would say come in, but that would be redundant," she snapped, and marched stiffly into the Gold Saloon. She sat down, but Monstuart remained on his feet, the better to intimidate her.

"I understand congratulations are in order, Miss Hermitage."

"You refer to Sir Darrow?"

"Precisely."

"I shall relay your congratulations."

"Save your breath. The congratulations are for you, not the gullible old fool."

"I must object to that, sir! He is eminently sensible, and not all that old either."

"He's old enough to be your grandfather."

"No, no. Only my father. He was a good friend of Papa."

"He's ancient!"

It was rapidly apparent to Sally that Monstuart's temper would not be so violent at her mother marrying an ancient. He thought *she* was Sir Darrow's bride, and his anger revealed a rampant interest in the fact. Why should he care whom she married, unless ... The situation appealed strongly to her sense of humor. "That is hardly any concern of yours," she replied with a careless toss of her curls.

"I have no concern whatsoever whom you ensnare in your toils, except when it comes to my nephew."

"Derwent?" she asked in perplexity.

"Don't try to deny you convinced that innocent idiot to marry your sister to provide you with a respectable house from which to make your bows. You succeeded, due to my negligence, but I'll be damned if you'll now get your money back."

Sally's amusement was swiftly congealing to angry confusion. There was a flavor of truth in his first accusation, enough to make her uncomfortable, but as to demanding money back, she was at a loss. "I have made no attempt to do so."

"Have you not? The boy doesn't draw a breath without your approval. If you think to shame me into repaying his debts, incurred to amuse *you* and further *your* financial ends of marrying money, you are out in your reckoning."

His tirade was largely ignored while she tried to make sense of it. "Has he dunned you for money?" she asked blandly.

"Only fifteen thousand pounds, a sum that is familiar to you, I think. He finds London unaccountably dear." His dark eyes toured the lavish room before settling on Sally's expensive gown.

"So that's why he has decided to go to Gravenhurst!"

"Derwent has had the scales removed from his eyes at last. He wishes to escape. I would like to know how even you, with your lavish spending, have managed to squander fifteen thousand pounds in less than a month."

Her eyes snapped. Anger with Derwent was included in her emotions. He should still have six thousand pounds! What was the wretched boy keeping from her? Gambling seemed the culprit, and gambling immediately brought forth the name Peacock. She naturally had no wish to let Monstuart know it. "You credit me with too much ingenuity in spending, milord. You are forgetting the matter of an extremely ugly sapphire tiara. At least my acquisitions are pretty and will be used occasionally."

"Used to trap an old man into financing you. I think you might have done better for yourself, with a little patience."

Sally leveled a dark look at him. "If I have a vice, I agree it is impatience. For some reason, which we shall not go into, the gentlemen seemed a little hesitant about coming forward this season. Don't think I was conned by your stunt. I know perfectly well why you tried to keep them away, and when that ploy did not fadge, why, you suddenly began dangling after me yourself. You were afraid I'd make a good match. It was all spite."

Monstuart's brows drew together in confusion. "I am not so devious as that!"

"Are you not?"

"With a little more patience, you would have learned that was not my plan. And I thank God for your impatience. To think I might have made the inalterable mistake of offering to marry you."

In the heat of anger, she paid little heed to his admission and thought only of a set-down. "I am less prone to mistakes of that sort. I would not have accepted any such offer, I promise you."

"Then you have obviously failed to determine from Derwent the exact total of my assets. I cannot believe your fondness for gray hair would have deterred you from accepting my offer when you knew what I am worth."

"I wouldn't marry you if you owned—a—a mint!"

"Don't let your sensitivities be perturbed by any fear of receiving an offer from me. I'll leave you to Sir Darrow. Will you *really* be able to stomach having that white-haired old man in your bed?"

Her cheeks flamed at his broad talk. "All cats are gray in the dark, folks say."

"You would even sink to that, giving yourself to a wizened old lecher for money. By God, I thought there was a grain of pride in you, but I was mistaken."

Sally jumped to her feet. "I have pride enough that I won't listen to these insults in my own house."

Monstuart rounded on her, eyes blazing. "You'll listen to what I choose to say, madam, in my *nephew's* house, if your mother ever hopes to recover a penny of her money. A very good case can be made that Derwent was defrauded."

"Unlike you, Derwent has some scruples. He would not drag his wife's family into court."

"You have discussed the possibility with your solicitor-groom, no doubt."

"That was unnecessary. It is only common sense. You have uttered your futile threat, milord. Withhold Derwent's money. Darrow will be happy to indulge the expensive taste of my family while you are the butt of the town's laughter, taking out your revenge on me by sending your own nephew to the cent percenters to be skinned alive."

"He hasn't an inch of skin left on his body since you got hold of him."

The iniquity of this charge robbed Sally of rational thought. To see Monstuart's snarling at her with unveiled hatred while he insulted her in every way imaginable was the last straw. She hardly realized what she was doing when her hand rose and struck at his arrogant face. A loud whack echoed in the room. She stared with horror as his face froze in shock. In that white face, a pair of furious eyes blazed like fire. His hands clenched to fists with the effort of controlling himself.

Her chest rose and fell in agitation, and her complexion was blanched bone white. "Get out of this house," she said in a voice trembling with fury.

"I will never willingly darken your door again. A gentleman must choose his friends with *some* discretion."

On this uncompromising speech, Monstuart turned and strode from the room. Sally heard the front door rattle on its hinges, and saw through the curtain Monstuart's retreating back. In his state of upheaval, he forgot his curricle was waiting and walked down the street.

Before she had time to recover, Melanie and Derwent came down the stairs and joined her. "Was that Monty's voice I heard?" Derwent asked.

Sally rounded on him. "Why did you ask him for fifteen thousand pounds?" she demanded.

"You know we are going to Gravenhurst. I wanted to repay your mama before leaving."

"We haven't spent the whole lot."

Derwent looked at his bride, and Melanie flew to his defense. "He never would have played cards with Peacock if *you* hadn't introduced him to us. He is a Johnnie Sharp."

"That's Captain Sharp, Mellie" was Derwent's contribution.

"He fleeced Derwent of every penny. And what Peacock didn't get out of him, his friend Hendry did. We had to ask Monty for money."

Sally turned her anger on Derwent. "I told you not to play with that creature. I warned you a dozen times. How much did he get?"

"All of it," Derwent said. "Er, what was Monty's answer?"

"His answer was no," Sally informed them.

As the full ramifications of her discussion with Monstuart rolled over her, she felt the unaccustomed prickle of tears stinging her eyes. Pride forbade shedding them in front of anyone, so she turned and whisked upstairs.

Melanie's lower lip began trembling. It never occurred to her that tears were to be hidden. She turned her moist eyes to her husband. "What are we going to do now, Ronald?"

"Go home with our pockets to let. Rusticate. Repay your mama gradually, a bit at a time."

"It's not fair. It's your money. I think you should speak to Monstuart yourself."

"From the way the front door was shaking, he was in a foul temper," Derwent pointed out.

"Give him an hour to cool down. His rages are soon dissipated. Mama wants her money. If she doesn't get it, she'll come to cuffs with Sally, and Sally will end up coming with us."

Derwent considered which was the worst of these eventualities and, after the hour was up, decided to tackle Monstuart. He went to his uncle's house and was shown into his private office, where Monstuart sat with a bottle of wine at his elbow and a small blue velvet box, brought back from Berkshire, on the desk in front of him. He was reviling himself for that romantic dash home to get the engagement ring and prepare the nest for a bride. He was not by any means disguised, but there was a whiff of the fox about his condition.

Monstuart looked up, wearing his most satirical face, and said, "So, Cawker. She has sent you to add her appeals, has she? The answer is no."

"I wish you will listen to reason, Uncle."

"I have never heard anything resembling reason issue from your lips so far. I doubt I will hear it now, but by all means deliver the lines Miss Hermitage has rehearsed for you."

"Sally don't know I'm here. I'm not under her thumb."

"And not letting her ride you into the ground, either," Monstuart snapped. "She's going to bankrupt you, and you, like a maw worm, let her do what she likes with your money."

"Now see here, Monstuart, Sally has nothing to say to anything. I spent the blunt myself."

"I haven't seen any new horseflesh or carriage or even a new jacket all season, but I've seen several fancy gowns."

"Well, I ain't paying for them."

"Then what have they done with your money?"

"I spent it myself. Sally didn't even know it was gone till I told her, just before I came here."

"Spent it on what?"

"I daresay you'll hear it anyhow. You can't sneeze in this town without the world knowing it. Peacock won it from me."

"And Miss Hermitage—did she know you were playing with Peacock?"

"Lord, no! She warned me from him—not that I ever would have met him if it weren't for her!"

"Don't hide behind a lady's skirts. It is even more odious than being a gudgeon. This took place at Brody's parlor, I assume?" Derwent nodded sheepishly. "After urging brandy on you?"

"Exactly. I say, Monty, did they fleece you, too?"

"No, and they shan't fleece any other innocents either. It's time to—" He batted his hand impatiently. "If Miss Hermitage wasn't even aware of your loss, why is she marrying Willowby?"

"Eh?"

"I thought it must be a shortage of funds that catapulted her into this hasty wedding."

"What the devil are you talking about, Monty? Melanie's *mother* is marrying him. They've been close as inkle weavers forever. He was her flirt years ago, before the family ever left London. Not that I mean to say there was anything irregular in it."

"Miss Hermitage has been running all over town with Willowby, with no sign of her mother."

"Mrs. Hermitage has gone to Ashford to sublet their house, and Sally is helping Sir Darrow arrange the wedding and buy the ring and all that. Good lord, you didn't think Sally would have that old bleater! I mean, she's a bad-tempered shrew, but she's too good for *him*."

Monstuart picked up the blue velvet box from the

desk, looked at the ring, and snapped the box shut. As he folded his fingers over it, an assessing light lit his eye, and over his lips there came an unsteadiness.

"I say, Monty, is that the family engagement ring you have there?"

"No," Monstuart lied easily. "It isn't."

"It certainly looks like it. Well, about the money, Monty—if you could see your way clear."

"Sue me." His uncle grinned. Then he put his head back against the thronelike back of his chair and laughed till his nephew thought he had run mad. When sanity and a feeling of peace returned to Lord Monstuart, he resumed speech.

"On second thought, perhaps I can do a little something for you. I am most eager for you and Lady Derwent to repair to Gravenhurst, and it would look bad for you to be walking so far. We'll discuss it tomorrow morning, Derwent."

"I will be home this evening, if—"

"No, I think I'd best give her the evening to simmer down. And I have a little business to attend to on Poland Street."

"Mellie won't be in a temper. She is very docile."

"I wasn't talking about Mellie."

"I see. Are you *sure* that wasn't the family engagement ring?"

"Things aren't always what they seem. I've just learned that lesson myself. Run along now, Derwent. I'll speak to your man of business and call on you tomorrow morning. You may tell Miss Hermitage I shall be there."

Derwent left. "May tell" didn't necessarily mean "must tell." Why should he suffer another bout of Sally's tongue?

Chapter Fourteen

Sally took dinner in her room that evening. It was Derwent and Melanie who greeted Mrs. Hermitage upon her arrival from Ashford and related all the incidents of Monstuart's visit. "First he refused point-blank to give us my money, but I was in touch with him later, and he is reconsidering," Derwent explained.

"He always likes to reconsider everything, does he not? I hope he will do something for you, Ronald, but if he doesn't, I shall speak to Darrow. He will arrange something. Where is Sal?"

"In her room, breaking vases and throwing books."

"Oh, dear, she is in one of her tempers. I suppose I should go up to her," Mrs. Hermitage said, and sat down to fan herself.

It was half an hour later when she went upstairs to change and peeped in at Sally's door in passing. It was clear at a glance that Sal was in one of her tempers, which rose higher as she recited her tale of Monstuart's visit. Her mother listened, then said,

"Ronald heard from him, and he is reconsidering giving him some money."

"Yes, as he reconsidered allowing the match in the first place. We've heard that story before! How dare he think I was marrying Sir Darrow!"

"You used to tease him about Mr. Heppleworth at Ashford. Perhaps he thinks you have a taste for older gentlemen. I don't see why that should put your nose out of joint. The important thing is that he is rethinking Derwent's money."

"When did Ronald hear from him? No message has come here." She had left her bedroom door ajar on purpose to monitor the front door messages. Of course, it was not any message to Ronald she had listened for. Monstuart must have learned his error by now. Surely he would apologize to her.

"Perhaps Ronald picked up the note at his club— he mentioned he had gone out. He told me definitely Monstuart is reconsidering. You are in such a pelter, Sal. Why do you not stay home this evening?"

"I feel fine, Mama."

"We are only going to a concert of antique music. I shall be so very busy tomorrow, preparing my wedding, that I want an early evening."

"I shall go with you," Sally said firmly. A concert of antique music suited her very well. The people there would not be Monstuart's close friends, but word would seep back to him that she had attended the concert with Sir Darrow. As her supposed engagement bothered him so much, she was eager to prolong his error.

During the concert she could be as morose as she wished, without looking any different from the rest of the audience. But when Sir Darrow took them for dinner after at the Pulteney, Sally came to life again. She laughed and chatted inanely while watching the entrance to see if Monstuart came in. He did not, and by the time Sir Darrow took them home, her head was splitting.

Mrs. Hermitage had one consolation from the evening. Just before she went up to her room, Sally said, "Would it be possible for us to cancel our ball, Mama? We are so busy at this time with the wedding that I have not attended to all the details. The cards haven't gone out yet, and as Mellie and Derwent are in a hurry to leave, it seems pointless to detain them two weeks for the ball."

"That's a good idea, Sal," Mrs. Hermitage said blandly.

"We'll have a ball later, Mabel, you and I and Sal," Sir Darrow added.

After Sally left, Sir Darrow said, "Sal seemed a bit off tonight."

"She had a terrific set-to with Monstuart."

"I noticed the black clouds hovering around him as he was calling on her. Money again, was it?"

"No, Darrow. It was you. The idiot took the idea it was Sal you were marrying."

"Ho, that explains it. Told me to go to hell. Jealous, then, is he?"

"Jealous?" Mrs. Hermitage looked shocked at the idea. "Good gracious, no, there was never anything between those two. They are too much alike to ever rub along. It is an old grudge, dating from Sal's arranging to nab Derwent for Melanie."

"Why should that consign me to hell? The pair of them were smelling like April and May at the

Engleworth ball. Several people mentioned it. Thought a match might be brewing. Not a bad idea to get her bounced off, Mabel. I mean to say—are we to honeymoon *à trois*?"

"No, we are not to honeymoon at all. We cannot leave Sal unchaperoned. Derwent and Mellie don't want her at Gravenhurst, and I most surely do not want her on our honeymoon. I thought after the Season is over we might billet her on some relatives for a month and dart to Paris."

"She couldn't do better than Monstuart," Darrow said pensively.

Mrs. Hermitage took a deep breath and girded her loins to duty. "She is my daughter, and I love her, Darrow, with all her little faults. I would not condemn her to Monstuart's keeping, not if she has to stay with us till she dies."

"Just a thought," he said. The thought stayed with him. A man didn't tell you to go to hell because he despised the lady he thought you were courting. "Sorry for your trouble, old chap," he'd say. Or "You're making a terrible mistake, old man." Wouldn't say "Go to hell." No point. "We'll be asking him to our nuptial soirée?"

Mrs. Hermitage drew a deep sigh. "We must, for Derwent's sake. That is exactly what I dislike so much about Monstuart. I am always having to be polite to him. If I could cut him for once, I would not dislike him so very much."

"You'll drop him a card, then."

"I shall give it to him tomorrow morning when he comes to give Ronald his verdict." After a moment's consideration she added more brightly, "Perhaps he'll have a previous engagement!"

184

"Very likely," Sir Darrow said, but he thought otherwise.

Sally had been informed that Monstuart was to call the next morning. She was in two minds regarding her own presence at that visit. "I will never willingly darken your door again" sang in her brain. When Derwent said, "Monty told me to let you know he would be here," her decision was made. He was hinting her away during this one necessary visit. A trip to Hatchard's for some books was her unimaginative errand. Unsure at what hour Monstuart was to call, she left at nine forty-five and prolonged the visit till after twelve by stopping at the shops.

She saw Monstuart's curricle drawing away from the house as she arrived home. Monstuart raised his curled beaver and called, "Good Morning, Miss Hermitage. Lovely day."

He was not overly dismayed when she lifted her chin in the air and purposefully turned her head the other way without replying. With the invitation to the nuptial soirée in his pocket, he knew he would see her soon.

Sally knew by the three smiling faces awaiting her in the Gold Saloon that Monstuart had opened his pockets. "What happened?" she asked eagerly.

"He got it back for me!" Derwent crowed. "Went straight to Brody's parlor and had it out with Peacock—in public."

"What do you mean? He got your money back?"

"Absolutely. By Jove, I wish I had been there," Derwent continued disjointedly. "Monty sat down to cards with Peacock and caught him red-handed, pulling an ace out of his sleeve. He let on he was

185

bosky, you know, to fool Peacock. He grabbed up the shaved cards for evidence as well. He challenged Peacock to a duel—naturally Peacock weaseled out of it, after all his boasting of having killed three men. He gave back my money, and I repaid Mrs. Hermitage. Monty has reported the establishment to Bow Street, and it is to be closed down."

Miss Hermitage refused to be impressed by this feat of daring. "Then he didn't actually give you any of your own money?" she asked haughtily.

"He's raised Derwent's allowance to seven thousand and paid Mama," Mellie told her. "And when Ronald is twenty-five, of course he will come into the whole thing."

This sensible plan received cool approval. Mrs. Hermitage added that Sir Darrow was agreeable to subletting the Cavendish Square house for the Season, so everyone's financial difficulties were straightened out. Sally disliked to ask the matter of greatest interest but was not long in doubt as to Monstuart's attendance at the nuptial soirée.

"I shan't mind having him here tomorrow evening, now that everything is straightened out." Mrs. Hermitage smiled.

"He accepted, then?" Sally asked without so much as a trace of pleasure. It seemed he had rescinded his intransigent stance regarding willingly entering the house. His presence was by no means necessary. If he came, it was because he wanted to. And if he felt safe to come, obviously he no longer considered her a threat to his freedom. She had lost the power to attract him.

"Most eagerly. He said he would not miss it for a wilderness of monkeys."

"What would anyone want with a wilderness of monkeys?" Melanie asked.

"What *is* a wilderness of monkeys?" Derwent added. No one, including Sally, could enlighten him.

"Could I speak to you a moment in private, Mama?" Sally asked.

They went into the study. "I have been thinking about your honeymoon," Sally said. "I cannot remain here alone, and naturally I do not mean to intrude on that private trip. Gravenhurst is not so very far away. I shall go there with Mellie and Derwent till your return."

"Oh, no!" her mother gasped. "They would not want—that is, we are not going on our honeymoon just yet, Sal. We have decided to put it off awhile. Sir Darrow is very busy right now."

Sally knew she was no favorite with Derwent, but to hear it blurted out so emphatically pained her. "They would not want you." That's what her mother meant, and she was right. They didn't want her. Her own mother couldn't possibly want her on her honeymoon. She had become an albatross around the necks of her family. This Season in London, so long anticipated, had become a punishment. The rest of her life seemed to offer no surcease. She was still a solicitor's dowerless daughter, and thanks to Monstuart's efforts, her reputation as an expensive woman was also well known.

"Perhaps I could visit friends in Ashford," she said, but half-heartedly.

Mrs. Hermitage was quick to scotch this plan. "You will never catch a husband there. Heppleworth has taken up with Nora Crosby's cousin—they are quite a twosome. The thing to do is for us to take you to all the balls and hope that someone will offer. Mr. Parkes speaks of you often. He is well to grass. The lack of a dot wouldn't bother *him*. Sal! Our wits are gone begging. I could speak to Darrow. He might be agreeable to my giving you the money I have left as a dowry. He is not at all clutch-fisted. Fifteen thousand—that is a perfectly respectable dot. It would open up new possibilities for you."

This was perfectly true, and very generous, but it brought no real pleasure to Sally. She simulated gratitude and expressed all the joy she should be feeling. Yet when she went upstairs, her heart felt like a large boulder in her chest. She didn't want an old man like Parkes to buy her, and she didn't want to buy a husband with her mother's money. She wanted Monstuart, free and clear.

She had always wanted him; since his first visits to Ashford she had felt a strong attraction. Knowing his faults, his pride, and his arrogance and propensity to lightskirts, she wanted him still. She lay on her bed, thinking. Was Lady Dennison really his mistress, or only a political cohort? He had cared for her good opinion when he had told her about the political meetings. Perhaps he had lied. Certainly he was a womanizer, or Papa would not have had to handle that case for him. She would never know the details of that intriguing business.

Whatever Monstuart's faults, he was too good for her. He was right to accuse her of managing Derwent, and doing the job poorly to boot. This rush wedding was her idea. And Derwent's acquaintance with Peacock was her doing as well. Why had she ever given Peacock the time of day except to make Monty jealous? The same urge had let Monty think she was going to marry Sir Darrow. Then his true opinion of her had come pouring out. He spoke of Derwent "having the scales removed from his eyes" and meant himself. He actually thought her so avaricious that she would marry an ancient, as long as he had money. His verdict was hard. He thanked God for his rescue from her clutches and spoke of the "inalterable mistake" of offering for her.

Her anger stirred again at these charges. There was no pleasing the man. He complained when he tricked her into behaving with propriety at Ashford, and again when she behaved like her sinful self in London. What did he want? And who was he to be so demanding? In a final fit of revolt, she rose from the bed, determined to put Monstuart out of her mind and heart and life. She had been happy before she had known him, living her life according to her own philosophy. She would not try to change a hair for him.

Mrs. Hermitage had arranged an intimate family party for the evening. Sir Darrow was the only guest, and the talk was all of the future, the wedding tomorrow, and the more distant future. They spoke of family visits to Gravenhurst and perhaps a tour of the Lake District in the early autumn. None of them had been there, and all wanted to see the beauties of mountains and fells and water. Sally listened, trying to catch their enthusiasm, but she felt an outsider. It would be the two happy couples and her, alone, the troublesome spare woman.

When the door knocker sounded at nine-thirty, she gave a leap of alarm. Monstuart! He had come! Her face turned quite pale, but she said nothing. In a moment the butler came and announced that Sir Darrow's secretary was sorry, but he must speak to him for a moment about some case that was pending. Sir Darrow had to leave early to attend to some business details, and Derwent wished to go over the business papers Monstuart had drawn up. The three ladies sat on alone, discussing the excitement of the past months till it was bedtime.

The next day was a confusion of wedding preparations, with the coiffeur rushing from one to the other, presents and flowers and food and caterers arriving to throw the house into chaos. At three o'clock the minister arrived for the simple ceremony, and afterward the wedding party went to the Clarendon to enjoy the elaborate dinner. Between the dinner and nuptial soirée, Sir Darrow had his most urgently needed belongings moved into the house.

By eight o'clock everyone had changed into evening attire to greet the guests and performers. Sally was able to put off her white gown for this informal do at home and wore her favorite color, green. Her hair was carefully arranged, her small diamond necklace in place, and her smile determinedly bright.

"Licked to a splinter" was Sir Darrow's compliment when she descended the staircase. Long as she had lingered at her mirror, she was downstairs before the other ladies. "Have you got a kiss for your new steppapa?"

She kissed his sere cheek, and his blue eyes danced in pleasure. "I see you dragging about the place like a stray kitten, Sal," he said in a kindly way. "You must never feel you are not wanted under my roof. We shall have merry old times, Mabel you and I. A daughter is something new to me. You and Mellie are the only children I have. I'm in no hurry to lose you."

"Thank you, Sir Darrow." He shook his head. "Papa." She smiled.

As if on impulse, he looked at her with a curious look and said, "Did Mabel tell you what Monstuart said when he saw me coming out of here t'other day?"

"No."

"Go to hell. That's what he said. I was very civil to him. Made him welcome, told him you were planning to ask him to the wedding, and he told me to go to hell. I respect a man who speaks his mind. Strange, though, is it not? You don't suppose he was jealous of me? Ho, there's a good joke, his thinking you would ever marry an old pelter like me."

"Monstuart is never hesitant in speaking his mind."

"I fancy you'll hear a piece of it tonight. Ah, here is the bride." He went forward, arms out, to greet his new lady, and Sally went to the saloon to think over what he had said. Would she be subjected to another piece of Monstuart's mind? If he dared to cast a single slur on anything to do with her or this marriage or Derwent's marriage, she would unceremoniously empty her wineglass in his face.

That was her mood when Monstuart arrived, not the first to come but far from the last. His dark eyes scoured the room for Sally and found her staring boldly at him. She immediately tossed her head and turned away. If he began edging toward her, she edged in the other direction. Without ever precisely looking at him, she managed to know where he was and where he was going and was at pains to take evasive action. When the players began their show, she took a safe seat between Sir Darrow and Derwent. Thus buttressed, she got through the concert with no awkwardness.

At dinner Sally had arranged her place at the far end of the table from Monstuart, and on the same side so that he could not even look down the board at her. There was to be no dancing. At twelve-thirty, the crowd began to disperse, and she had not exchanged a single word with him. While she had taken elaborate steps to avoid doing so, something in her resented his lack of initiative. When he was one of the first to leave, she was ready to crown him.

In a fit of the sulks, she went into the vacant library and slammed the door behind her. She would not cry. She had a wonderful life to look forward to. Sir Darrow loved her like a daughter; he had agreed to giving her all of her mother's money for her dowry. The rest of the season would be better, and if she didn't find a husband this year, next year she would do better. In the autumn the whole family was going to the Lake District. Her future could hardly be brighter, or her effort to hold in her tears more difficult.

When she heard a tap at the door, she thought little of it, except to be grateful she wasn't crying. Monstuart had left, so obviously it was only some guest who had gotten lost in the labyrinth of the house, or perhaps it was just Mama.

"Come in," she called.

The door opened slowly, and Monstuart stepped in.

Chapter Fifteen

"I thought you had left!" Sally exclaimed.

"I did. I came back." Monstuart stood hesitantly at the doorway, waiting to see if she picked a book from the shelf and hurled it at his head.

"What do you want?" she demanded. He began to close the door behind him. "Please leave that open," she called imperiously, for no particular reason except to annoy him.

Monstuart left the door ajar and strolled warily toward her. "I thought the party was breaking up and I might return a little later and speak to you in privacy. As I have waited for a quarter of an hour and still the guests are hanging on, I decided to come back."

"The guests may be lingering, but I am eager to retire. What is it you have to say?"

He advanced toward her. Sally's lack of cooperation was swiftly eroding his good humor. "I came to apologize for my tirade the other day, when you let me believe you were marrying Willowby."

"I said nothing of the sort."

"You didn't correct my misapprehension. You knew what I thought."

"It's not my job to correct the many errors you fall into. You made your opinion of me perfectly clear," she charged. "From the very beginning you have done nothing but find fault with me."

"You are not completely innocent of the same charge. *I* was judged before I reached Ashford. It was my duty to protect Derwent's interests."

"A duty you took rather lightly, I might add, shearing off when you were supposed to be reconsidering."

"You weren't slow to push forward the wedding, behind my back. You only did it to get the better of me."

"What a monstrous ego! That wasn't the only—the reason."

A flash of triumph lit his eyes. "I am aware of the other reason—viz. to get yourself a Season. You have succeeded, so let us cease bickering about that."

"It's impossible to talk to you without quarreling."

Monstuart hunched his shoulders. "No matter, bickering is actually my manner of courting a lady. I assumed it was your way of receiving my attentions, to retaliate thrust for thrust. Come now, you must own it is more interesting than the conventional exchange of banalities. You know your hair is like a raven's wing and your eyes like emeralds, or whatever gemstone is in fashion this year," he said offhandedly. Sally peered from the corner of her eyes. "I know I am the manliest man you have ever met and, what you never would tell me, almost certainly the wealthiest."

"I would *never—*"

"Of course you wouldn't. I have just said so. Even among friends, I would be only the most eligible, not the plain Anglo-Saxon 'richest.' "

"I wasn't angling after your fortune, so don't think it!" she charged angrily.

"I acquit you of such sensible behavior. But pray, don't tell me you have not enjoyed our bouts of mutual insulting, for I don't believe it."

"I may have enjoyed bickering—a little—but it had nothing to do with courting in my mind. I like the insipid conventions very much. And no one ever told me I had hair like a raven's . . . wing. . . ." The words petered to silence.

"You have, if it gives you any pleasure to hear it. Only a curly raven's wing, of course." His finger flicked a curl over her ear. "Ravishing." The finger moved to brush her cheek. "Skin like marble, eyes like a panther's—and the sleek stride of one when you walk, too, all smooth and undulating."

"Monstuart! I cannot believe these are the conventional banalities."

"They are the similes that occur to me. I didn't mean to offend you. I admire panthers, especially their walk." Her marble face colored alarmingly as she stared at him from her slanted emerald eyes. "Dare I proceed with my compliments, or have you had enough?"

"That is more than enough," she said primly, though she was dying to hear more.

"I won't take it amiss if you care to find a resemblance to Adonis in me," he suggested playfully.

"Since we have lowered—raised—*altered* the tone of our conversation."

"Adonis! You're more like Bluebeard."

Monstuart rubbed his chin. "I shaved not six hours ago. My beard grows quickly. It is taken as a sign of virility among those of us who are cursed with it."

"I really must go now," Sally said.

"Will you be kind enough to give me some hint, before you leave, as to how I should proceed in future?"

"I suggest you proceed with more propriety, if you care for the good opinion of me or anyone else."

He nodded his head in agreement. "I care for yours. May I do myself the honor of calling on you tomorrow morning?"

After a moment's consideration, she replied, "If you will behave, you may."

"I shall make every effort to behave in a manner you think you will like, ma'am," he said. He bowed and walked toward the door. Before leaving he stopped and tossed over his shoulder, "But you'll be bored to flinders, Sal."

The next morning before she rose from the breakfast table, Miss Hermitage received a large bouquet of red roses and a box of bonbons from her "respectful suitor, Monstuart."

"What can it mean?" Mrs. Hermitage, now Lady Willowby, asked in confusion. "I am sure he hadn't a word to say to you last evening, Sal."

Sir Darrow's eyes twinkled merrily across the board. "Go to hell, ho! I knew he was jealous as a green cow."

196

Lady Willowby looked a question at Sally. "It sounds as though Monstuart must be in love with you."

"Love!" Sir Darrow smiled. "The young use that as an excuse for bad manners nowadays. Go to hell—imagine. In my youth, we behaved better with the ones we loved, not worse."

"I don't think it's *you* he is in love with, Darrow," his bride informed him.

"No, no. He was jealous of me. What do you think of that, Mabel, a top-of-the-trees buck like Monstuart jealous of your husband?"

"Don't be so foolish, Darrow. And eat your crusts."

Lord Monstuart arrived shortly after his gifts. Miss Hermitage received him in the Gold Saloon, with her mother playing propriety while Sally thanked him most civilly for his gifts. Lady Willowby took up her netting and moved discreetly to the far side of the room.

"I received the flowers and bonbons, Monstuart. Thank you very much," Sally said primly.

"I reconsidered," Monstuart replied, "and decided you were right. Some token obeisance must be made to convention so you may hold up your head among your family and friends. But let it be understood *entre nous*, Miss Hermitage, you are not to eat any of that box of disgusting sweets. Let Mellie gorge herself. She'll run to fat inside of a year anyway, but I don't want your sleek lines blurred. A pudgy panther, you know, would be a ludicrous sight."

Sally tried nobly to swallow her smile and look

offended, but her trembling lips gave her away. "May I smell my flowers?"

"By all means, but I don't want to hear of their going beneath your pillow, or into a book to be pressed. And if you try to stick one in my lapel, I shall throttle the breath out of your white marble throat."

"Just how great an effort are you really making to behave, Monstuart?"

"About as great an effort as I think will please you. None at all, in other words. We have endured one boringly civil evening at Ashford. I must congratulate you on your performance. You nearly convinced me you were a proper bride for Heppleworth. Why the devil did you do it?"

"To deprive you of an excuse to prevent the wedding due to my impropriety."

"It had quite the opposite effect. I had decided to permit the wedding and only withheld Derwent's money so you would have to continue seeing me."

"Monster!"

"Now the gloves are off. Let us get down to some serious blows. What did you mean by calling me a Bluebeard last night? I didn't find my chin shadowed when I got home."

"No, and didn't bother checking to see if it was, either."

"I did! I'm a little vain of my appearance when I'm courting. But of course you were alluding to that other gent, the one who killed all his wives and locked their bodies in a room. A singularly foolish method of disposal. Like Bluebeard, I will be happy to entrust the keys of my house to you. And unlike Bluebeard's Fatima, you may open any door you wish. My life is an open book. Not a dull one, either."

"I didn't assume it was, when you required my father's services on a delicate matter."

He shot a quick, sharp glance at her. "I sued a neighbor who decided he wanted to put a fence down the middle of my pasture."

"Papa did not deal in trifles."

"It wasn't a trifling fence—six miles long and ten yards inside my boundary. And not for a trifling fee either, I might add. I figure in twenty or so years I'll recoup what I paid the Hermit for the job. It served me right. I was green enough at the time to want the prestige of saying the Hermit was handling my affairs, and he was crafty enough to dowse me."

"I see no particular delicacy in a misplaced fence."

"You are your father's daughter. How does an elephant's memory fit inside a panther's head? I said my life was an open book, and I'll read you that unedifying chapter in toto, if you wish. I was—ah—negotiating with my neighbor at the time for his daughter, not in marriage, and he decided to see how far he could up the price. So I decided to show him."

Sally sniffed in displeasure. "The Hermit's daughter is plagued with another doubt. How does a neighbor who apparently owns some considerable lands dispose of his daughter, *not* in marriage?" Lady Willowby looked up at hearing the word Hermit.

Monstuart glanced at the mother but continued speaking in a normal voice. "When she has made herself a byword with her behavior, he is sometimes inclined to do so. I wouldn't want to give you the notion I am in the habit of ruining maidens."

"What a charming neighborhood yours is, to be sure. This chapter makes lively reading. The protagonists promise delightful company for your wife." The word "wife" caused another glance from Lady Willowby. Again Monstuart ignored the warning sign.

"He moved away. So did the daughter. An elderly couple bought the house."

"Such tediously respectable neighbors explain your lengthy holiday with Lady Dennison."

"I have told you about that."

Sally glanced at him from the corner of her eyes. "Is it true that politics makes strange bedfellows?"

"Probably, but in this case it has made no bedfellows that I am aware of. Now have you any chapters to read me?"

"We're not finished with the last case yet. The aforesaid daughter for whom you were negotiating—was the transaction completed?"

Monstuart brushed an invisible speck from his jacket shoulder. "It was, and so were a few others. I'm not a saint."

"Nor even a very faithful sinner, it would seem!"

He twitched impatiently. "It is my intention to be a faithful husband, and it is an intention that will pave no roads to hell—one I intend to keep, in other words."

"Surely that much is implicit in the word 'intention.' "

"Strange, I feel I've had this conversation before, with your father. He put many probing questions to me regarding my intentions in the aforesaid negotiation. There were redeeming features in the case. I mentioned, I believe, that I was a green and callow youth at the time."

"Many years ago," she slid in mischievously. "Would you say your book has taken a turn for the duller since then?"

"No, but I say with no fear or doubt that it will take a turn toward propriety if you will marry me. My wild oats are all sown." Monstuart regarded her steadfastly.

Lady Willowby was hanging on every word now. How did he dare to propose in a public room? Sally looked at her mother, then back at Monstuart, with an angry question in her eyes.

"I'm flattered, quite beside myself at your enthusiasm," he offered.

"You should be happy I don't beat you over the head with an andiron. How *dare* you propose in such a public place?" she hissed.

"It is the only place I dared to reveal my scarlet past to you, here, where I am safe from your claws—for the time being. I know your temper is not stable. I have found in the past that after the first burst of violence is over, you subside back into docility rather quickly. I am the same myself, and with the two of us falling into a fit of passion—angry passion, that is—simultaneously, God only knows what havoc we might create. You with your andiron and I with my strength and virility. Nothing would remain but hair and claws. There, I see your temper is subsiding already. What do you say to my offer?"

"What offer?"

Lady Willowby shuffled along the sofa, closer to them.

"Dear elephant, your father would despair of you. You missed the most important bit. Amid all that jungle of verbiage there was a definite statement of intent. The less legal-minded call it an offer of marriage. There should have been a profession of undying love and devotion as well, I expect. Pray consider it said."

Sally took a deep breath. "Lord Monstuart, if you think to escape the banalities entirely, you misjudge your quarry."

"Oh, excellent, Sal! You never disappoint me. What a predatory, hunting interpretation you put on my decent offer."

"I expect you would like to hang a panther's head on your trophy wall, to boast to the world of your prowess, but if you think to get it with that offhand offer, you are mistaken. Derwent tells Mellie he adores her ten times a day, and what do I get? A box of bonbons I am not to eat, flowers I cannot press, and a casual remark that I may consider myself courted. Well, you, sir, may consider yourself turned off."

Monstuart listened with a bored expression. "So there," he said when she stopped to draw a breath. "Now I am turned off. I make a dash to find a new mistress on whose bosom I drown my sorrows. You become fiendishly jealous and have to go at some unsuspecting gent—Peacock, perhaps—no, you wouldn't like him with his daylights darkened. Better stick with the invalid. We are both desolate and realize—after, say, a week's remorse—that we have made a wretched but fortunately not irreparable mistake."

Sally turned and flounced across the room. Lady Willowby received a commanding look from her daughter. She picked up her netting and hurried out the door to tell Mellie and Derwent the news.

Monstuart strolled nonchalantly after Sally and continued speaking over her shoulder. "I come crawling back with my tail firmly tucked between my legs. We meet by careful chance on the street. I offer to carry home your fish. You accept—coldly, of course—but you deign to accept. At the door, I hint I could do with a drink. Your coolness begins to thaw. You relent and ask me in. Where would you like to hear your second proposal? Let's make it right here, since you have cleared the way for privacy."

Sally rounded on him. "I didn't ask her to leave!"

Monstuart grabbed her hands, tilted his head in an attitude of disbelief, but didn't contradict her. "Miss Hermitage, I realize I have offended you by my cavalier behavior in the past. Dare I hope—Oh, good, you're smiling."

Her lips trembled open in a smile. "You're incorrigible!"

His hands slid up her arms. "Insensitive, inconsiderate, incoherent, insane, in love." His harsh face softened to something resembling gentleness. A lambent gleam glowed in his dark eyes, and when he spoke, his voice was husky. "What do you say, Sal?"

"I'll consider your offer," she said primly, her eyes dancing with mischief.

Monstuart nodded blandly. "I'll meet you on the strut tomorrow to tote home the fish. Don't make it a whale, to teach me a lesson, will you? Shall we say—elevenish? *A demain.*" He bowed and walked into the hallway.

Sally stood, unable to believe he had actually left. She ran into the hall after him and was pulled into his arms. "I couldn't wait either," he said. "I have been wanting to do this since I first laid eyes on you."

He crushed her against his chest and lowered his lips to hers. Her eyelids fluttered, and beneath the lashes he saw a gleam of uncertainty that thrilled him more than passion. His kiss was gentle, till he had calmed her alarm. When she began to warm to his embrace, it firmed to demand. Soon she was being mauled in a most satisfactory manner. During a brief hiatus in their embrace, Sally pulled away and looked at him from eyes glazed with love.

"I bet you haven't even spoken to Papa—Sir Darrow, I mean."

"I'll stop in at his office and tell him. I have a ring I meant to bring along as well, but I forgot."

"Monty!"

With a laugh, he pulled a large diamond ring from his pocket and slid it on her finger. "Consider this as a set of manacles."

"Mellie got a tiara, too. You only had Derwent buy it in order to squander Mama's money, didn't you?"

"Of course I did. How else was I to get power over you?"

"I knew it!"

"You read me uncommonly well, Sally."

She put her arm through his and led him off to tell her mother the news. "Bear in mind, milord. Between my mind-reading and my short temper, you shan't get away with a thing."

"I'm under the panther's paw now."

He looked remarkably pleased with this perilous position, and so did Miss Hermitage.